Clarity

NICOLE DYKES

Copyright © 2020 by nicole dykes

All rights reserved.

No part of this book may be reproduced in any form or by any electronic or mechanical means, including information storage and retrieval systems, without written permission from the author, except for the use of brief quotations in a book review.

❀ Created with Vellum

This book is dedicated to anyone who feels so lost they don't believe they can ever come back. Have faith. Take a deep breath. Soon everything will become clear.
Also, to anyone who ever felt damaged by someone else's cruelness, remember every child is precious and should be treated that way. Embrace the good and keep going forward, don't let the bad win.

Playlist

Push

Matchbox Twenty

River

Bishop Briggs

You And I

Lady Gaga

Die Wild

Dia Frampton

Tired Of You

The Exies

I'm With You

Avril Lavigne

Into The Fire

Thirteen Senses

Paralyzer

Finger Eleven

I Love Me

Demi Lovato

July

Noah Cyrus

Young

Livingston

Some Kind of Disaster

All Time Low

My Songs Know What You Did In The Dark

Fall Out Boy

Stubborn Love

The Lumineers

Lost Boy

Ruth B.

Jar of Hearts

Christina Perri

Goodbyes (ft. Young Thug)

Post Malone

No Rain

Blind Melon

What's Up?

4 Non Blondes

I Don't Believe You

Pink

New Slang

The Shins

Hallelujah

Pentatonix

Runaway Train

Soul Asylum

You Found Me

The Fray

Half A Man

Dean Lewis

****I don't own the rights to any of these songs, but I listened to them as I wrote this book. They all have a deep connection to Blair and Rhys for me.*

Rhys

PROLOGUE
7 years ago

"It was a dream," I gasp into the night air. "It was a dream."

I try to catch my breath.

It. Was. A. Dream.

I can't breathe. I can't fucking breathe.

I sink down to the sidewalk, the cement digging into my knees, clawing at my collar as I try to catch my breath.

I want it to be a dream, but the sickening feeling inside tells me it wasn't just a nightmare.

It was my life. My reality. My bleak existence.

I look back at the rundown apartment building I've been staying in, stealing shit and hustling with my friend Sean to get rent money even though we're both still in high school.

I had to get out of there. I'm not even safe in my own bed, no matter where the bed is located.

And now, I can't fucking breathe.

I need a fix. I need to go numb and not remember. Because when I remember, I can't breathe. I can't function.

I reach into the pocket of my sweats, pulling out the cellphone I lifted from some yuppie who didn't need it.

I should call Sean or Quinn.

Fuck. Quinn. She hates when I use. Maybe I could get lost in her, but the high doesn't last nearly as long as the drugs.

No. I can't call her. I've hurt her enough. She's my best friend and my occasional girlfriend. We all grew up together. Sean, Quinn, me . . . and Logan, but that fucker left us behind for a better life.

A better man would be happy for him, but I'm not. I hate him. I despise him for becoming what we all hate. The rich and privileged. Above the law. They can buy their way out of anything. They can have anything they want. And now my best friend since long before we reached puberty is living with them.

I call my dealer, giving him my location and hang up. I sit on the cement, feeling the hardness and the cold. I'm only wearing a thin t-shirt in November, but I don't care about the cold. I grew up in the cold. I was raised in black numbness.

I don't want to think about waking up in my bed covered in sweat only moments ago. I don't want to think about how badly my body needs a hit. I can't think about a better time because there wasn't one.

I just want it all to stop.

Rhys

I WAKE up and stretch my arms which are tired from hours of lifting and punching the bag at the gym last night after my shift at the tattoo studio.

It's a good tired, one I like.

I push the covers off and stand up, looking around my studio apartment located above the tattoo shop where I work. I'm grateful for this place, but I need my boss, Chris, to start accepting rent from me. I've been working for him for well over a year, and that's when he said he would start taking my rent check.

And although when he took me in, I was fresh out of rehab and broke as fuck, I've saved a decent amount now. But the guy loves to baby me, which pisses me off because I know he doesn't treat anyone else like that.

Technically, Chris Adamson is one of the privileged. He grew up in a wealthy family. But he made his own way, started a little tattoo shop that grew. And the man has talent. I'm lucky to have learned from the best.

I see my phone—one I bought and pay for with my paycheck—and swipe to see a text from Sean.

Your ass better be at the fuckin' party.

I grunt after I read it. Text back a quick "K" that I know will piss him off and toss it to the bed. Of course I'm going to be there.

My best friend. The man who never left my side since we were little kids is moving all the way to New York City tomorrow. *Fucking traitor.*

But he's a photographer, a true artist who has the opportunity to be great. And I will not hold him back.

I take a quick shower, get dressed, and go down the shop just as Chris is unlocking it. He smiles when he sees me. "Always the first one here."

I shrug my bulky shoulders. "I live upstairs."

He starts his normal routine of getting the shop ready for customers, and I go to my station. I just want to be left alone. That's what I always want and what I try my best to portray to all my co-workers, but they never play by my rules.

Case in point, Chris is sitting on my stool before I'm even done setting up. "I need to talk to you, kid."

Kid. He always calls me "kid," but I suppose twenty-three is a kid to a guy in his forties. "You firing me already?"

He grins. "No, but you do have to leave."

I stare at him, unsure about what the fuck is going on. "What are you talking about?"

He hands me something, but I don't look down at it. "I need you to move to St. Louis for me."

"St. Louis? What the fuck are you talking about?" I look down at the paper and see the word "DEED" at the top. "What is this?"

"Your own shop. It's a shithole, but I think you can do a lot with it."

What? I look down at the paper, seeing my name on the deed. Why? "No fucking way."

"Yes fucking way. You've earned it, kid."

"No. I haven't. And I don't need your pity shop."

He laughs because Chris has no problem laughing about anything. "When Logan first came to me and asked me to give you a job, I was skeptical like anyone would be. But you've stayed clean. You've done your job, and you have fucking talent."

It's bad enough I only have this job because when Logan took my girl, Quinn, and my balls, he made it even worse by asking his Uncle Chris to give me a job as a consolation prize. "I can't take this. Give it to Jay."

Jay, Ty, and Frankie are all artists who also work here and have long before me. They're like family.

"That fucker is never leaving here. Ty, Frankie, and he are now all my partners in this shop. But I want to open another shop. It's yours, but I'm a silent partner."

"The money."

"Just take it. Go. Be free, little bird."

Even though I'm thankful to him, and he's done a ton of shit for me, I still can't resist holding up my middle finger.

And the fucker just laughs.

I find myself watching Jay, Frankie, Ty, and him laugh often. I wonder how it comes so easy to them. How they can laugh about almost anything.

I don't laugh.

I rarely smile.

I've never seen a reason to.

"When?"

"I know we have a bigass party to attend tomorrow." Of course, it couldn't just be me and Sean to send Sean off. No, we have to include all Logan's bigass family at a fancy country club. Because that's who we are now. "So, how about the day after that?"

"That's fast."

"The shop has an apartment above it too. It's the exact same setup, Rhys. It's ready to go." He laughs. "Okay, that's a lie. It needs some work, but I have all the faith in the world in you, kid."

That should feel good, but it doesn't. I don't want anyone depending on me. Ever.

"I'll pay you back."

He laughs. Again. So fucking easy. "No shit. It's coming out of the profits. I'm not worried."

"You really shouldn't put this much faith in me."

"Rhys." He looks like he wants to pat me on the head or the

shoulder, but he knows better. I hate to be touched. And he respects that, his icy blue eyes locking on mine and making me uncomfortable. "You gotta start believing in the good in you. We see it."

I shrug. "Don't."

He stands up. "I'm gonna miss you, but I'll stop by. St. Louis isn't too far."

"Three hours."

He nods and goes back to the front, going about his day like he didn't just hand me, a twenty-three-year-old, punk kid, ex-addict a shop of his own.

I didn't know people like him existed when I was growing up.

I still have a hard time believing they do.

Blair

I stare at the tattoo on my wrist, a cloud with a lightning bolt coming out of it. I trace over it and smile, thinking about Logan's words to me.

"You just need a man strong enough to weather the storm who needs a badass bitch to go through it with him."

That was the day I asked him to give me a tattoo. He wouldn't because he didn't love me. He was always in love with Quinn and, like every other man I knew, he was just using me. Until he found her again.

It's fine. Quinn is cool, and we actually all still stay in touch. Quinn has become someone I go to often to just chat about nothing and everything.

And then I think about the man who actually gave me this tattoo. I feel the bitterness rise in my throat, thinking about our last interaction. Then I turn to look at the man, snoring and fast asleep next to me.

Red hair. I don't remember that.

Whatever.

As slowly as I can, I slip off the bed and start to look around the room—which smells like gym socks and pizza—for my clothes. No more college bars.

I'm twenty-three. I need to be looking for older men, but I refuse to fully embrace my daddy issues.

I find my skirt, and quickly slip it on, searching for my top. I finally find it on top of the dresser, but it catches on a baseball bobble head which crashes to the ground, waking the stranger who sits upright, looking at me groggily. "Are you leaving?"

I pull the tank over my bare breasts and nod. "Yeah. I need to get to work."

He runs his fingers through his hair, his arm muscles flexing as he does. *Not bad. Not great.*

Not nearly as sculpted and hard as the arms I want to hold me.

"Don't you work for your father?"

"Yes." I remember telling him that over drinks at the bar last night before we came back here for lame, at the very best mediocre, sex.

"So, can't you tell him you're going to be late?" He looks down at his lap, and I see the tent he's making in the sheet. "I could definitely go for another round after seeing your tits in the sunlight."

I nearly gag, hating that this fucker has seen me naked and touched my body. But no regrets. I can't start allowing that. I don't want any part of round two and would love to just get the fuck out of here, which is exactly what I'm going to do.

"I could, but not for a skinny, little five-inch dick."

I reach for the door and pull it open. I hear him mumble, "Bitch," but I don't care. I'm already out of his room and out the front door.

Besides, I've been called worse.

I look around. Shit. Of course, my car is still at the bar. I reach into my pocket for my cellphone. Normally I would just call my best friend, Melody, but I'm sure she's busy packing, considering she's moving to New York with Sean tomorrow.

I quickly order an Uber and sit on the curb to wait. Looking down at my phone, I see a message from Mel about the party tomorrow, making sure I'll be there.

I wouldn't miss it for the world even though the thought makes my stomach twist into knots.

CLARITY

I know it's a big party, but that's not what bothers me.
Rhys will be there to send Sean off.
And it's a party, just like the one tomorrow, where it all began.
Where we began, even if neither of us knew it.

Blair

Two years ago

THAT PARTY WAS BORING as fuck. Growing up at country club parties, it just doesn't thrill me. Not to mention watching my best friend lust after a total prick who's going to hurt her.

When I first went to Rhys earlier tonight at the Christmas Eve party, my only intention was to find Sean and threaten him for hitting on Melody and messing with her head.

But there was something about this boy, who's definitely all man, something different. *Dirty. Sexy. Angry.*

He's definitely a change from the men I've been fucking since Logan tossed me aside.

I thought Logan might be different. He was raised in foster care on the other side of the tracks, so to speak, but he was in love with a girl from his past.

Oh well, Rhys seems like he can occupy my time just fine for the night. I toss my keys on the foyer table as Rhys stalks in behind me, closing the door.

Perhaps I should be a little afraid of him—I mean, the man is massive—but I'm not. I have zero fear as I turn around to face him, ready to fuck him. I approach quickly, placing my hands on his shoulders ready to kiss him, but he flinches.

And I don't mean slightly. I mean full-on flinches like I burned him with my hands. He steps back out of my grasp and stares at me, horror in his eyes.

"What's the matter?" I stare at the beautiful man dressed in a tux that clings to him but still seems completely wrong. His thick brown hair is gelled. His cheekbones are high, cut, and sharp like glass. His eyes burn with hatred in them, an all-consuming hate, and I'm not sure where it's directed. His lips are bright red and full. Sexy. And I want to taste them.

"Don't touch me."

I raise one eyebrow in his direction, placing a hand on my hip as I watch him. Is he fucking with me? "So . . . you thought I was bringing you back to my house so we could what? Watch TV? Talk about our hopes and dreams?"

He grunts, his voice hoarse, deep, and serious, "I don't fucking talk either."

"Great." I try not to roll my eyes because he looks homicidal now, but seriously? What the fuck? "So, no talking and no touching. This sounds like a great night." My voice is dripping with sarcasm, and I don't care.

I think back to our conversation at the party right before we left to drive here.

"You wanna get out of here?" I'd asked. I mean, hey, he was hot and broody.

"Didn't you just threaten me? And my friend?" he'd asked. And yes, yes. I'd done that, and I'd do it again. Sean better not hurt my friend.

"This party is fucking boring, and you look like a halfway decent time," I said back. And I meant it. He looks like he can fuck.

"You can't handle me." That was his warning. His warning that made my panties fucking wet. I was on the hook after that, wanting him to destroy me in the best way, barely able to wait until we got to my place.

"I'm not scared." And I wasn't, not at all. I was excited.

"I won't stay," he said. And of course, that only got me hotter. I'm

not looking for anything serious. I don't want love. I want a dirty, hot fuck.

"I won't ask you to," I assured him because I won't.

"I won't call," he said, again trying to scare me away.

"I won't even give you my number," I'd answered because why would I? I don't plan to ever see him again.

He told me to lead the way as if that was exactly what he fucking wanted. And now we're standing here, both fully clothed, and he won't let me touch him.

I stand before him, studying his handsome face, dying to see what he has under his tux. Melody says I'm like a guy when it comes to sex, always wanting it and not afraid to make that known. But I say I'm just a woman with a healthy sex drive who isn't afraid of that. Who the hell decided guys were the only ones who could like sex?

"Look, I promise I can make it feel good." My hands start toward his thick chest, but he steps back again, looking wounded. Again, I gape at him in astonishment. "So, we came back here to fuck, but I can't touch you?"

"I don't remember ever saying we were going to fuck."

"It was definitely implied." I'm not the crazy one, right? He looks tortured as he looks at me in my golden gown.

I sigh, and maybe I've figured it out. "Look, you don't have to do this to prove anything. You really don't."

His eyes meet mine, confusion in them. "What are you talking about?"

"Let me guess, your father was a really macho, tough guy type. He would never accept his son being gay. God forbid you like to fuck men, right?"

He stares at me, brow furrowed. "No."

Not really a talker, this one. But it makes sense. I get it. He's beautiful, almost too pretty for a guy, but I think he's ashamed of that. He wants to be ugly. He's quiet because he has a secret, one that shouldn't be a big deal. But because of his father, he hides it. "I understand, Rhys. Fuck him. He can't dictate who you fuck. You don't need to stick your dick in a copious number of women just trying to prove to daddy that you're not gay."

Again. No fucking words. It's maddening.

"My touch repulses you because my hand is attached to a body with tits."

"That's not it."

"It's really okay..."

"Jesus, fuck. Stop talking." Again, I should probably be a little afraid, but I just stand, arms crossed, one foot in front of the other and wait for an explanation. His tattooed hand slides over his face, looking pained. "I wish I was into dudes. They talk less."

I glare at him and then let my eyes slide down lower, down to the crotch of his black tuxedo pants. "Is it a dick problem? Like deformed or something? Uncut?"

"What?"

I shrug. "I don't mind that, I guess. I've only seen one."

"What the fuck?" When I look up, I see he looks horrified again. "You just asked if I'm not circumcised?"

He's wound so damn tight. "Yeah, I mean the one I did see... the guy was really self-conscious about it."

"I'm cut."

My eyes drop back down. "Small?" I lift my eyes back up to his. "Because that's fine too." I try to hide my laugh, but I swear I'm serious. "As long as you know how to use it."

"Fuck. You're talking again."

"Well, we aren't fucking."

He takes another step, but this time it's closer to me instead of further away. "Is that what will shut you up?"

I bite my bottom lip, my heart racing from his presence. "Yes." I step closer but don't touch him yet. "Tell me what you like, Rhys."

"Quiet."

"Hmmm..." I turn away from him and point to my zipper. "I'm kind of a screamer."

I'm surprised when he takes the hint and lowers the zipper to the top of my ass, dragging it down slowly but not lingering once it reaches the end. I slip one arm out of the gown and then the other. I'm not wearing anything underneath. It's too form fitting for that.

"That doesn't surprise me."

I lower the gown to my waist and cover my breasts, turning back around to face him. His eyes don't drop down to my chest like I would expect. "So, I can't touch you?"

"No," he growls simply, his voice dripping with sex and sin.

I drop my hands to the dress bunched at my waist and finally his eyes drag down, looking at my tits but not saying a word. Still, I see it there now.

Desire.

I shimmy out of the dress, leaving myself completely bare for him with the exception of my designer heels as I kick the fabric away. "But can you touch me?"

"I don't know." It's sheer torment. Not just for me. I can hear it in his voice. Uncertainty. Like he isn't sure if he can.

I take his wrist cautiously, and he starts to jerk away, but I hold on and place his hand on my left breast. I let go of him but can feel the weight of his hand on my skin. "Not so bad, right?"

HIs other hand reaches up, cupping my other breast as I bite my lip trying not to make a sound. It's strange, but I don't want to spook him.

I'm used to hearing how beautiful I am and how great my tits are. They are pretty great but paid for. I'm accustomed to guys telling me what they want to do to me. What they want me to do to them. Admiration and lust. But Rhys doesn't say a word.

His thumbs circle over my hardened nipples, and my breasts are rising and falling with my rapid breathing.

I have no idea what it is about this man, but his touch doesn't leave me bored or empty. I want more, crave it even.

"Touch me, Rhys," I whisper softly.

His eyes meet mine, and I try to move forward for a kiss, but he shakes his head in a warning, making me groan with need.

Then he drops to his knees, his hands on my ass, and I look down at the beautiful man before me.

He doesn't lock eyes with me. Instead his eyes are locked between my legs, staring at me. *There.*

I gasp, and my head falls back when I feel his tongue make contact with my wet slit, dragging slowly up to my clit. "Oh my God."

His fingers dig into my ass, adding to the pleasure of his mouth. His tongue swirls over my clit at an almost punishing rate. He's not taking his time with me.

Does he just want it to be over?

My hands grasp his shoulders, and he winces, pulling away from me, and I groan as I realize my mistake.

I hold my hands up as I look down at him. "Sorry. I won't touch." There's a little sarcasm in my tone, but he doesn't care. He resumes licking my pussy, focusing mostly on my clit, not letting up.

I keep my hands off him even though I'm dying to touch him, to know what's under that tux, to strip him bare and find out what he's hiding.

Scars?

Maybe.

I wouldn't give a fuck with a tongue like this. "Oh God, Rhys," I gasp, my body flying toward an intense orgasm.

I want my fingers in his hair. I want to grasp the strands and pull, but I don't. I don't want this to end.

I'm so fucking close and settle on cupping my own breasts in my hands, pinching my nipples and adding to the pleasure this mystery man is giving me.

"Fuck! Rhys, right there." *As if he doesn't already know.* He's been focusing on the right spot the entire time.

He doesn't fuck around.

I come, and I mean hard, my hands gripping my breasts with punishing pressure, knowing I can't touch him.

He laps at me, giving me every last drop of pleasure before he stands up and takes a step back, wiping his mouth.

I move toward him, pressing my breasts against his chest. He hisses but doesn't push me away. "Let me touch you." I can't believe how desperate I sound.

My hands slide over his sides, and he doesn't pull away, but he does close his eyes like he's in pain.

He's breathing heavily, but I don't think it's because he's turned-on. I press my lips to his throat, kissing and sucking, trying to get him to stay here with me, trying to get him to let go. But suddenly his fingers dig into my arms, and he moves my body away from his.

He doesn't say a word while I stare at him.

Instead he turns away from me, moving to the door, opening it, and walking out. He closes the door behind him, and I stand there, naked and alone.

Wondering what the fuck just happened.

Rhys

B*LAIR*.

Jesus Christ. Does she ever leave anything to the imagination?

Of course, since I saw her completely naked the first time I met her, I can close my eyes and see every inch of her anytime I want.

Her body is as close to perfection as you can get.

Long tan legs only made more perfect by the high heels she's wearing. The backless dress hits above the middle of her thigh and hugs the curve of her perfectly round ass. Her hips are flared, but her waist is tiny. Her tits are full, almost too big for her frame, and the dress doesn't hide them. It dips low and is sleeveless, showing off her smooth tan arms.

Her long blond hair is down, falling to the top of her breasts. Her makeup so flawless, you'd swear she wasn't wearing any.

A living, breathing Barbie doll. Except this one has a serious bite along with her beauty. She'll rip your balls off and keep them as a trophy.

I should know.

"You're staring." Fuck. I turn to look at Sean whose bright white smile is blinding.

I just grunt, tired of explaining. "Where's your wife?"

He nods his head toward a group of women at this "party." A

party with no alcohol because those who can drink are outnumbered by children and addicts.

"You're really leaving?"

He nods once, but I see how certain he is. "Yup. Come with us."

He knows I won't. "Can't. I just got my own shop."

He looks shocked but thrilled. "What? You motherfucker. You're just now telling me?"

"I just found out. I leave tomorrow."

He laughs, and it's fucking joyous and almost contagious, but I don't laugh. "That's so great, man." He slaps an arm around me, and I flinch, but not enough to make him move his arm. He's the only one who gets away with it. "Look at us."

Quinn and Logan walk to us, joining us, and I smile when I see Quinn's belly has started to swell. He knocked her up.

And they couldn't be happier. They flew in this morning and fly out tonight. Their home is in Nashville where Chris gave Logan his own shop and a start.

"Hey, mama. Can't believe you let this guy put a baby in you," Sean says as he grabs her for a hug. She smiles wide and bright, beaming.

Sean and Logan shake hands. Old friends.

All four of us come from the same background. They all got out. They're all happy.

Which is as close to happiness as I'll ever come, but it's good enough for me. Quinn stands in front of me, offering a smaller smile. She doesn't touch me even though I would let her.

"Hey, Rhys."

"Hi, Quinn." I thought she was my one chance at happiness. I thought maybe dating her could free me from all the shit, make me forget. But it wasn't meant to be. She's always loved Logan. She never loved me.

"You look good."

"You look better." She smiles, and Logan wraps an arm around her. I don't hate him anymore. The better man won. I treated her like shit when we were together, and he treats her like something precious that he should protect.

The way I should have.

"Blair's here?" Logan seems surprised.

"Melody is her best friend," I say, not sure why he thought she wouldn't be.

He nods his head, shrugging. "I thought she was moving."

I feel a tug inside my chest with that information but try to keep my cool. "Blair's moving?" I turn to Sean. "With you?"

"Fuck no." He shakes his head emphatically, still not a huge fan of Blair, and the feeling is mutual.

"No, she's going to St. Louis."

I'm pretty sure my jaw just dropped, and I hate showing any emotion, but it makes Quinn smirk. "St. Louis?"

She nods, watching me with amusement. "Yeah. She's going to run her dad's company there. It's a sister company to the one here in K.C., but apparently, it's having some issues."

I hate how close they are now. You would think Quinn would fucking hate Blair. I mean, Blair used to fuck Logan. But no, they're best fucking friends.

She's moving to St. Louis. I look across the room, catching her glare. She's definitely still pissed-off at me.

Good.

"Well, fuck. Life has more jokes."

They all look at each other, and then I feel three pairs of eyes on me. It's Sean who connects the dots and bursts out in laughter. "Oh, fuck. Your new shop is in St. Louis?"

"Keep laughing, motherfucker."

"Oh, I am." And he does, which makes Quinn and Logan laugh in confusion.

Quinn's eyes meet mine. "You got a shop?"

"Yeah. In St. Fucking Louis."

Now Quinn and Logan are cracking up along with Sean, and I raise both middle fingers, leaving the fucking laughing hyenas behind.

I can still hear them laughing.
Fuckers.

Blair

God, he looks good.

The asshole.

It's not fair.

He's not in a tux or even a suit. Apparently he dressed in the bare minimum to get into the country club. A pair of khakis and a polo. The polo hugs his massive biceps and shows off the full sleeve of tattoos on his right arm and the tattoo on his bicep on his left.

He's solid muscle covering broody angst.

I hate that my body craves a taste of him.

I finally pull my gaze away from Rhys when I see Mel approaching me, dressed in pink, her innocent face made up sweetly. And that really is what Melody is. Innocent.

We may both be blond, rich bitches, but she's my opposite.

Believes in love. Wants the best for her friends and family. So fucking forgiving and kind.

It would make me sick if she wasn't like a sister to me. And okay, yeah, sometimes it still does even though I would gladly commit murder for her.

"I'm so happy you're here!" she squeals as she gives me a big hug.

"Bitch, like I would miss it."

"You're a little late though."

Yeah, I'm super late. I didn't want to be here. I didn't want to face the fact that one of my best friends is leaving. I don't know how to deal. But I finally got my ass dressed and showed up. "I'm sorry, Mel."

She's still smiling brightly. "It's okay. You sure you won't come with me?"

I shake my head from side to side. "I don't think I have the patience for New York. I'd probably kill someone."

She laughs, so fucking used to my attitude. "Probably."

"Besides, my dad transferred me to his St. Louis office, so I'm moving there in a few days."

Her jaw drops, and again, she looks so pure and innocent, easy prey for the wolves. Which is exactly what Sean was at first, but I guess they're happy now.

So, I guess I'm happy for them. I am happy for them, but I'm still watching him. I trust no one.

"You didn't say anything."

"You've had a lot going on. And besides, I only found out a few days ago." When my father told me exactly what was going to happen.

"Are you excited?" She would be. Melody loves any change. It's an adventure for her. Me? Not so much.

I shrug. "It is what it is. It's pretty much Kansas City anyway. They're sister cities."

She nods her head just as Quinn, Logan, and Sean join us. I'm not sure where Rhys went. Sean wraps an arm around her. "We have to get going. Don't want to miss our flight."

She gazes up at him, so fucking happy. And then she sighs, looking at me. "I'm going to miss the hell out of you."

I hug her tightly. They're all riding to the airport together.

There's officially nothing left for me in Kansas City. "I'm going to miss you too. Call me. Stay safe. And if anyone needs their balls removed, I'll be on the next flight."

I eye Sean, who playfully shivers as Mel squeezes me tighter before finally letting me go. I give Sean a hug and whisper in his ear, "You know I'm talking about you."

He nods easily, brushing it off. "I won't ever hurt her."

"Again," I add because I'm a bitch.

"Again." He smiles and then guides his wife toward the car. I give Logan and Quinn quick hugs before they make the rounds and leave.

The party goes on, but all I see is Rhys, who is still here.

And I know why.

I'm not in the mood to celebrate losing my best friend to New York. I'm not in the mood to mingle and make small talk.

But I am in the mood for him.

Rhys

Two years ago

"Hey, kid." I look up from my sketchbook, alone in the breakroom and see Jay's big ass crowding the door frame. "Customer is asking for you."

He wags his eyebrows at me so I know it's a chick. And a hot one.

He's always trying to get me laid. Which is annoying. And kinda creepy. But the guy means well.

I climb up from the couch and walk to the main area, instantly seeing Blair.

No. Fuck.

The last time I saw her she was naked and flushed from the orgasm I'd just given her, but I didn't fuck her like she wanted. That was almost a month ago.

I felt like a freak, staring at her naked body and unable to let her touch me.

My entire body is tense as I approach her. Damn, she looks good. Way too good.

She's wearing jeans, a white shirt, and a black leather jacket. It should be a simple look, but on her, it's anything but simple.

"Rhys." Her lips slide up into a sly smile. Cunning.

"Blair. What can I do for you?"

I feel Jay's eyes on us, and I'm silently imploring him not to say anything.

Her small shoulder kicks up. "Logan pussied out when I asked him to give me a tattoo, so I thought maybe you could."

I nod curtly. "Sure."

I move to lead her toward my chair, but she stops me. "Wait. Don't you guys have private rooms?"

I turn to look at her, wondering what kind of fucking game she's playing. "Do you need a private room?"

I can feel Jay smirking at my side. "Oh yeah, pretty girl. We have private rooms."

Fuck.

I shoot him a dirty look, but he clearly doesn't give a flying fuck. I lead Blair to the private room but leave the door open.

She shrugs out of her jacket, leaving her in a tiny white t-shirt that should be fucking illegal. She's wearing a white bra underneath, but it hides nothing.

"Blair . . ." My voice is a warning.

I don't trust this chick.

I don't trust anyone.

"So, you really *are* always this uptight." She's studying me, and I don't like it.

"Yes." I ready my station and sit on the stool next to her. "What do you want?"

She licks her lips, and I roll my eyes, knowing exactly what she wants.

"Are you always this fucking over-the-top horny?"

She just laughs, tossing her head back and showing off her pearly whites. "Yes."

"I'm not going to fuck you at work."

She turns to her side like the chair is a fucking bed, tucking her hand under her head to prop it up and look at me. "But you will fuck me?"

"Jesus, are you in heat?"

Again, she laughs. She shouldn't. I'm not joking. I'm an asshole who's already sick of her shit. But then she gets serious on me. "Honestly?"

I give a nod. She says, "I've never had anyone treat me like you did."

"You mean made you come?"

Her pretty eyes roll. "No. I've come many times by other hands. But only once with a tongue. That was hot."

"You talk way too much."

She doesn't laugh this time, just eyes me. "I mean, you didn't fuck me. You didn't want to?"

Christ. I drag a hand over my eyes and blow out a puff of breath before meeting her eyes again. "Is this about your ego? Is that it? Worried your pussy didn't taste good? And that's why I bailed?"

She shifts in her seat, looking surprised but not full-on shocked. "That actually never crossed my mind."

"It did," her eyes meet mine with a question, "taste good."

And it did. Fuck, I wanted to bury myself so far inside her after that. But I fucking couldn't.

She visibly swallows, and I can see her nipples poking through her white shirt now. She really is turned the fuck on.

"So why didn't you want to fuck me?"

"If I tell you, will you tell me where and what you want tattooed and get the fuck out of here after I'm done?"

Her eyes narrow, and she's thinking it over. "Yes."

I'm not going to tell her everything. Fuck that shit. But I'll give her enough to shut her up. "I'm an addict. Heroine. Cocaine. Alcohol. You fucking name it. I'm an addict. But I've been sober for a couple of years." I grab my tattoo gun. "And I've never fucked sober before."

"Oh." That's all she fucking says, which I find strange. The way she talks nonstop, I figured she'd have a million questions after that declaration. Everyone is always trying to make me talk. But she just settles back in her seat, holding out her wrist to me. "I want a storm cloud on my wrist."

I stare at her in astonishment but thinking that was way too easy.

"Okay."

I get to work, tattooing a cloud with a lightning bolt striking out of it onto her delicate wrist. She doesn't say another word until I'm finished, but she's staring at it.

"That's perfect."

I want to ask her why she wanted a fucking cloud. But I don't.

"You can pay up front."

"What time do you get off work?"

My eyes slide to hers. "I should have been off thirty minutes ago."

Why did I just tell her the truth?

She nods, slipping her jacket on her small shoulders. "So you wanna try again?"

"Are you for real?"

She smiles, feigning innocence. But I know there's none left, and I prefer it that way. "I won't laugh if you can't get it up." She stands up. "And if you end up only going down on me again, well, good for me."

She winks. I shake my head, but I almost feel a tug at the corners of my lips.

She's something else, this one.

Unlike anyone I've met.

"Okay. I live upstairs. Come up when you're done. There's an entrance around back." The last thing I need is the guys knowing I'm upstairs with Blair.

I go upstairs through the shop, and before I know it, she's knocking on the other door.

Fuck! I don't know if I can do this.

I open the door, my heart thundering in my chest as she walks past me, not letting her small body touch mine as I close the door behind her.

I turn to face her, and she takes off her jacket, throwing it and her purse to my couch. "So how can we do this with you sober?"

I swallow, feeling absolute fear. Fear I can't stand.

"I don't know."

It's the truth. I've always had to be high or at the very least drunk to fuck someone. *You know whiskey dick? Yeah, I have the opposite problem.*

She stalks closer to me, and I feel a coat of sweat fall over my body. My nerves are out of control, and I want to bail. I want to run down the stairs and find a quick fix.

"Relax." Her voice is soothing. "I won't touch you."

I give a curt nod as she lifts her shirt over her head, leaving her in a lacy white bra that doesn't do much to contain her full tits. I should be hard.

Painfully so.

She's fucking gorgeous.

"Take off your shirt. Let me see you," she commands, and I growl with a shake of my head.

"Rhys . . ." Her hands reach back to the clasps of her bra. "Bare chest for bare chest."

Somehow the challenge is one I can accept, and my hands go to the hem of my shirt, lifting it up and off. She removes her bra, and we're left staring at each other. Unmoving.

My throat feels dry as my eyes slide over each perfect breast, round and full with already puckered dark rose nipples.

"Now pants?" she asks. She actually seems nervous as her hands move to the button on her jeans.

"I'm not wearing underwear."

She smiles at that and shrugs her shoulders. She kicks off her boots before unbuttoning her pants and pushing them to the ground, leaving her in a black lacey thong. "Now? Cock for pussy, even though I've already showed you mine."

And I've tasted hers.

The thought actually stirs my dick to life. I almost can't believe it when I look down. I can feel her eying me with curiosity. I mean, clearly I'm fucked-up, but she's not running. She just stands in front of me, not touching, only looking. Her gaze does something crazy to me.

"I don't care. I really don't."

"Care about what?"

Her eyes slide over my abs to my crotch then slowly back up. "If it's small. Or looks weird. All dicks kind of look weird."

She thinks I'm shy? Or self-conscious?

I almost fucking laugh. *Almost.* I run my hand through my hair and look at her pretty face.

If only.

"I'm not worried about how my dick looks." I'm worried about it not fucking working. I'm worried about flipping out when I press into her. I'm worried about fucking feeling what I don't want to. Of remembering things I don't want to. Of so many things.

"Rhys." Her voice is sultry as fuck, and it actually goes straight to my dick which twitches in my jeans, dying to get free.

"Now." Before I chicken out. I kick my shoes off and grab my socks, removing them and staring at her as my shaky fingers move to the button on my jeans.

Her fingers find the strings of her thong, and I take a deep breath as we both remove the last bit of clothes shielding us.

I stand still, my eyes on her face as hers dip lower, looking slightly surprised. But then she meets my eyes. "You have a nice dick."

Again, this chick almost makes me smile. "Are you really that surprised?"

"Yes. You were acting like you had a tiny little thing when it's actually kinda monstrous."

"Thing?" I take a step closer to her.

"Cock. Dick. One-eyed—" I hold my hand up to stop her, and she laughs. "I can keep going."

"I believe you."

"So, what are your rules, Rhys? Can I suck your cock?"

Her eyes move down where the tip of my dick is glistening with need at that idea, but honestly, I think it's a bad idea. Too fucking intimate somehow.

Don't ask me how my twisted up brain works. "No."

"You're seriously turning down a blowjob?"

"Yes."

She bites her bottom lip with curiosity again. She's trying to figure me out, find out what I like. She probably thinks I'm kinky as fuck when in reality, I'm not playing a game. I really can't stand to be touched when I'm sober.

"Okay." Her voice is low, almost a little shaky, and it's oddly exciting to me. I know this isn't a girl who gets rattled often. "Do what you want to me."

That should not be a turn-on.

I walk toward her, my body stalking to hers, and she takes a step back. "Second guessing?"

She shakes her head, but takes yet another step back, meeting the wall near the exit. "No. Do you have a condom?"

I walk to the dresser by my bed and grab one, walking back to her.

"I mean, you're probably clean anyway. Not having sex for a couple of years. And I always make guys wrap it up."

I lean in close to her, careful to keep my lips away from hers. "You're talking again."

She swallows her nerves. And that's exactly what this is. She's nervous.

I didn't think that was possible.

"I'm clean." I open the condom wrapper and slide it onto my cock that, remarkably, has stayed hard. "But I'm not looking to be a dad. And I don't trust you."

"I don't trust you either, fucker." Now she's defensive. "And I'm not fucking stupid. I don't want to be a mom. I have an IUD."

"Good."

I'm still leaving the condom on. She could be a twisted bitch for all I know.

"Don't touch me."

She nods her head and lifts her arms above her head, plastering herself to the wall. The movement pulls her tits up even higher, and she looks hot as hell waiting for me to fuck her, to do whatever I want to her.

Her eyes are on me though, sending my heart racing as my dick touches her thigh, and she shivers with need.

I can't do this.

I can't fucking do this.

I can't breathe.

"Rhys. Don't make me beg."

"I can't do this." God I'm such a pussy.

She thinks for a moment, and then without dropping her hands she swivels her entire body, facing the wall. Somehow knowing the eye contact was a problem.

"You're better than this. You aren't a fucking sex doll." I mean, I'm assuming she *is* better than this. Fuck, anyone deserves better than this.

Her small shoulder lifts, "Make it feel good, and I won't care."

What happened to this chick to put up with this shit from me? It's all I can think as I use my foot to nudge hers to the side, spreading her legs wider for me, and I enter her. I'm not gentle. I'm not fucking sweet.

I'm brutal.

It's the only way I know how to fuck. Just get to the finish line.

She cries out at the intrusion, but she moves her hips back toward me, accepting each punishing thrust. Her body doesn't retreat from me, it moves with mine.

"Fuck, you're big."

I stop moving. "Don't say that."

She doesn't look at me. Thank God. I can't handle it while I'm buried inside her. Her pussy clenches tightly around me, and she moves her hips back, urging me to move. She doesn't say another word as I continue fucking her, my hands braced on the wall next to her head.

It's ridiculous being inside her and still afraid for my body to touch hers, but that's how she made this possible.

That's how, minutes later, I'm coming. And then, she's coming around my cock, screaming my name when she does.

She wasn't kidding about being a screamer, but I don't think she was faking with the way she was clenched around me.

I pull out of her and stumble back, walking to the bathroom and disposing of the condom. Hoping like hell she's gone before I come back out. But of course, she's not.

She's getting dressed and tosses me my jeans. I catch them.

"That was oddly hot."

I stare at her as she pulls her jeans on and then her shirt, followed by the jacket. She grabs a piece of paper and a pen out of her purse, quickly scribbling something on it and leaving it on my couch.

"I guess I lied."

I look at the paper and see a phone number.

She winks as she opens the door. "Call me sometime. I wouldn't mind doing that again."

Is this girl for real?

Blair

My hands are planted firmly against the stall in the bathroom at the country club as I close my eyes and focus on Rhys's cock thrusting deep inside me.

Nothing has changed.

Everything has changed.

I don't touch him. We don't talk. I don't look at him.

HIs hands grip my hips as he continues to impale me with his giant dick. And I love every single second of it. I let my head fall back and wait for the orgasm to come. Because it always does with him.

I'm frustrated from the weak lay the other day. Somehow, even if I've never been able to feel his body or look him in the eye while he fucks me, Rhys still knows my body well. His cock presses against that perfect spot inside me over and over again, and I feel it. The tingle runs through my entire body, my fingers want something to grab, but instead I just ball them up into fists against the stall door.

Don't ask me how we got here. It wasn't difficult. All it took was a look from both of us after our friends left and it was on. Because Rhys doesn't use words, and I've gotten used to that. Even if I hate him. Even when I'm so fucking angry at him I could scream. It doesn't matter.

I'm leaving. I needed to say goodbye the only way we can.

Pathetic? Maybe.

But I don't care. I learned a while ago that when it comes to this hulk of a man, I'm pretty damn pathetic.

When we finish, he removes the condom, tossing it in the trash and zips up. I know there won't be any words. There rarely are with him.

I tug my skirt back down and exit the stall before even looking at him. I make my way to the sink and wash my hands, making sure to spend a little extra time after touching the stall door.

He washes his hands next to me at the sink, and it almost feels intimate. Us standing at a double sink.

"I'm moving."

"I heard." Of course, he did. And of course, he isn't going to say anything else because why would he?

I don't mean shit to him. He's made that pretty fucking clear.

Maybe I don't even have a right to be mad at him. I knew exactly who he was the first time we hooked up. He hasn't changed.

I have, and I have no idea when I turned into this chick. Desperate to hear a man tell her he'll miss her. Hell, that he'll miss fucking me. *Anything. Jesus.*

But no. Nothing.

I dry my hands and then turn to face him. "Well, thanks for another great fuck."

I start to leave, but he catches my arm. I look at the spot where his hand is on my elbow, and like an idiot, I actually take pleasure in the touch.

Jesus, what the fuck did I let him turn me into?

I yank out of his hold, and he just stands there, looking at me with the dark expression I'm so used to. "What?"

"Be careful."

I snort. "I'm not scared of anything, Rhys."

"I know."

Two-word sentences. His forte.

"Have a nice life, Rhys."

"You too."

Fuck! I grab the door handle, so pissed-off I want to take it out on someone. I want to slap the shit out of him and shake him. Beg him to wake the hell up from his daze. I want to scream at him. Make him listen. But I can't touch Rhys.

Not physically and not in any other fucking way.

I thought I was hard to love, but Rhys is stone.

Rhys

I LIVE in St. Louis now. This is fucking weird. Quinn and Logan are in Tennessee, living their own lives with new friends. Logan has a few guys who work for him at his shop. Sean is in New York with Melody, a spoiled little rich girl. I can't fucking believe he landed one of those. I think that was always his dream, although I've never understood it. And I'm here. I thought I'd stay in Kansas City forever. Hell, I thought we all would. But the shop Chris bought isn't bad. Not bad at all, really.

It's located downtown and is a little hole-in-the-wall, nearly mirroring the shop in Kansas City. It will just be me for now. I'm not looking to hire anytime soon. Or maybe ever.

I like the quiet.

I've only been here for a day, but I've started to clean up the place. It needs work. A lot of work. The place is fucking rough. Even the front glass doors were broken, shards of glass spread out all over the place when I got here. I know Chris could have afforded a place that was already finished, all sparkly and shit, but he knows me better than that.

I appreciate this more. Actually having to work for it. At least when it's all said and done, I might feel like I earned it and a little less like this was charity. I can't stand anyone's pity.

He budgeted for repairs though, the fucker, and even though I have some money saved, he made me use it for supplies. So I ordered everything I'd need. Bought paint and materials to redo the floor because it was shit.

I'll have clients before I know it because Chris has a solid reputation, and for whatever reason he's willing to put that on the line for me. And there is no way in hell I'll let him down.

As I sand down the marred parts on the wall and apply putty, I think about Blair and yesterday in the bathroom stall. You would think fucking in a bathroom would feel dirty, but not at the country club. That bathroom is cleaner than any I've ever been in.

She could be in St. Louis by now for all I know. I didn't ask her any questions. I already knew she's moving here. I never ask questions. I let people tell me whatever they want me to hear. It works out better that way.

I've found most people want to talk. But Blair is fucking stubborn.

She was pissed. I know she wanted me to say so much to her, but I can't. Or maybe I won't. I don't know.

She seems to think it's the latter. That I just don't want to talk about anything real. Not even to her. Like she's something special.

She seemed so safe at first, but then, it finally became clear she's far more dangerous to me than anyone else.

Rhys

Two years ago

It's been a month since I fucked Blair in my apartment above the tattoo shop, and I'm still stunned it happened. That my dick was hard and stayed hard the entire time. Hell, it stayed hard even after she left.

No alcohol needed.

Just her.

It's really fucking crazy. I've been staying clean. Going to meetings.

But as if she already knew, she comes in through the front door of the shop with that fucking smirk on her pale pink lips. I've been having new cravings.

I stand up, not letting Jay get to her first, not giving him a chance to let me know she's here in his own clever little way that I won't find funny.

I stand inches from her, out of anyone's listening range because of the music playing in the shop and the sounds of the tattoo guns. "What are you doing here?"

My tone comes out almost playful. At least for me. "I need a tattoo. Know anyone who can do that for me?" Her eyebrow lifts, and I swear everything this girl says drips with sex.

"You don't have to get a tattoo every time you want me to fuck you."

She doesn't flinch. Not even a little bit. Instead she laughs easily. "Good to know, but I really do want a tattoo first. I've looked like a damn Barbie doll my entire life." She shrugs, and I almost smile at that because she's not wrong. She definitely resembles the doll but with a serious edge. "I might as well be Badass Barbie."

And I know she added the "first" to let me know she definitely wants to fuck me. She makes it easy for me. Easy is something I've never really had. My entire life has been layered with complicated.

"Private room?"

She nods her head. "Of course."

I lead the way and leave the door open. I don't want her getting any crazy ideas. I'm not fucking her in my place of work.

Only above it.

She takes her jacket off and then lifts her shirt off, leaving her completely bare. "Fuck." I close the door, and she laughs and sits down in the chair, settling back.

"Jesus, do they have to be leather seats? That's fucking cold."

"Then put your shirt back on," I growl as I sit on the stool next to the chair and try my best to remain professional.

Don't look at her tits.

"I can't. I want my tattoo right here . . ." She points to her side right next to her right breast.

"You can leave your shirt on. Or you could have worn a bra."

She just shrugs. "Don't get all shy on me now, Rhys. You've seen it all before."

Every fucking time I close my eyes.

"This is my job."

She gives me a no-nonsense look. "Then do your job."

It's going to be difficult with my dick trying to escape my jeans, but I guess I should thank her for the hard-on. Seems my dick is used to her now. Not only that, it wants to fucking own her.

"What tattoo?"

"A rose."

I tilt my head to the side, cocking an eyebrow. She doesn't seem like a flower girl. I can't tell you how many flowers I've tattooed onto chicks.

She just shrugs, totally unbothered by my judgment. "Beauty and the Beast was my favorite movie growing up. So, sue me."

My eyes lock on hers and she sucks in a surprised breath as if connecting some dots I'm not aware of. "I've never seen it."

Now she's looking at me like I'm a fucking freak, and yeah, maybe I am. I was nearly an adult before I had my own television, and believe me, I wasn't watching Disney. "Never?"

"Never. I know what it is though. Disney," I grunt with disgust.

Her eyes roll. "Yes. Disney, and don't fucking give me that look like I'm a little princess watching silly cartoons. Anyone who grew up watching Disney will tell you that's the most depressing shit you'll ever watch. Almost downright depraved."

I show her several roses, and she picks one. "Depraved? Disney?"

Again, with the fucking rolling of her eyes. "Yes. Beauty and the Beast. The Beast was a beautiful, spoiled prince who had a spell cast on him, turning him into this hideous beast. And the Beauty? She was this sweet, innocent little bookworm, a dreamer who traded herself for her father when the Beast held him captive." I start to work as she continues, not flinching at the needle. "And of course, at first, she's totally repulsed by him and afraid, but then she gets Stockholm syndrome and falls completely in love with him."

"With her captor."

She nods her head. "Totally. I mean, the dude did have a kickass library and talking furniture. So, I get it."

"You're ridiculous."

She laughs. "But when they fall for each other. When she loves him, seeing the good inside him, that's when he turns into the hot prince again. But it's pretty fucked-up."

"Sounds like it."

"Definitely. And then Snow White? I mean, holy fuck. Her stepmother tries to have her murdered because Snow White is prettier than her. Then she shacks up with seven dudes until she's poisoned, and the only thing that can bring her back is a kiss from a prince."

"Sounds fucking stupid."

"Oh, for sure," she agrees and laughs again. "Honestly, all Disney did was teach little girls that a prince would come and rescue them someday, which is definitely fucking stupid. They never tell you that princes really just want to stick their dick in you until they get bored."

I stare at her, and her eyes widen as they meet mine. I don't think she meant to get so deep. And I'm definitely uncomfortable as she shifts in her seat. "Stay still."

She nods and shuts up. And oddly enough, I miss her voice babbling on.

"But you still like it?" *Enough to get a tattoo of it.* Even though I still have no idea what the rose has to do with the story, I'm not going to ask.

She lifts her shoulder. "At least she kind of made him work for it. And he was a surly bastard for everyone else but her. I kind of like that."

I finish, and she looks down at my work.

"Thanks."

I nod and start to tell her where she can pay, but she silences me.

"Pay at the counter. When are you finished?"

I look at the clock. "Ten minutes."

"See you then."

And sure enough, when I clock out and go up to my apartment, she's waiting for me at the outside door. I let her in, and she strips off her jacket, tossing it to my couch like she lives here. "So, you want to do something different this time?"

I know I look like a frightened kid right now, my eyes wide. My palms are sweating so much I have to wipe them off on my jeans. She just snickers as she stands right in front of me. She doesn't touch me though.

"Relax. I didn't mean touching you. I mean a different position."

"Oh." My throat is still dry as I stare at her. "Why are you being so nice to me?"

That really makes her laugh as she pulls her shirt over her head again, and this time I do look at her tits. Because they're fucking nice.

I lift my shirt off over my head, tossing it behind me because I know the game by now.

"First of all, I'm not fucking nice." She kicks her heels off, and I take my shoes and socks off. "Second of all, I think that's the longest sentence you've spoken to me, so congrats on that." I make an irritated grunt, but she just keeps going as we both push our jeans down, kicking them away. She removes her panties, leaving us both fully naked. "And third, you're a good lay with a big dick. And I've been fucking college boys who can't find my clit for way too long."

"You really are Badass Barbie."

She laughs again, effortless and free as she looks back over at my bed. "How about doggie style? That doesn't require eye contact or much touching."

I nod in silent agreement as she goes to my bed and I follow.

She really doesn't mind catering to my bullshit.

Or maybe I'm the beast to her beauty. Whatever, I'm just here for the ride.

Blair

I'VE BEEN in St. Louis for almost a week, and I'm fucking bored out of my mind. I mean, surprise, surprise, right?

I've always been bored with my own existence.

I moved into the house my father bought that was already fully furnished. I started working at his company like I was supposed to. I'm a bitch on the outside, that's how most people see me, but let's face it, I'm really just the dutiful daughter doing what I'm told.

I don't really go outside the box until it comes to fucking.

Somehow, that gave me a kind of control over my life. But it never changes much for long.

I'm annoyed by the hands on my hips right now, sliding lower and lower and then over my ass. He's grinding against me on the dancefloor, but I don't really want him to.

I don't not want him to either though.

I'm dying to feel even a small spark. Some kind of thrilling connection that will wake me from my boredom. But this dumbass behind me with spiky hair and a button-down shirt?

Yeah, it's not gonna be him.

I push his hands off me and make my way to the bar, ordering two tequila shots as I check my phone.

There's a text from Mel that makes me smile. She's sent a picture of Sean and her standing in front of their new apartment building. They look happy.

"I got it." I look over to see a guy dressed in a black leather jacket and tight jeans paying for my shots.

He has short hair, almost trimmed to his scalp, decently built.

He could do for tonight.

"Thanks."

His eyes glide down my body with absolutely no shame. "Wanna dance?"

I down both shots quickly and turn back to him. "Lead the way."

We move out to the dance floor, and he doesn't hesitate. Not even for a split second. His hands move right to my hips. Possessive. Hungry. "You're fucking gorgeous."

I place my hands on his shoulder and move my body along with him. He doesn't flinch at my touch. He doesn't push me away. He pulls me closer, and it should be hot. I should love that this guy runs his hands all over my body as we dance. That he wants me to touch him.

"Jesus, your body is insane." He shouts into my ear because the music in the club is really loud.

What a dumbass.

I just want him to shut the fuck up. I keep dancing with him though, letting his dick press against me. A promise of what's to come, and by the way he's dancing, I'm betting it won't be me.

So why do it?

I stare out into the crowd, searching for eyes that aren't there, for a man who can't stand for me to touch him.

Who only wants quiet.

And I drift back to the beginning of the end as I lift my hair and drop it slowly, letting it fall, and the guy grinds against me.

But I'm not here with him.

I'm there.

Blair

Almost a year ago

THIS HAS BEEN the trip from hell. Going on this road trip with Sean, Mel, and Rhys to see Quinn in concert was so epically fucking stupid.

I've hooked up with Rhys a lot over the last year. We've kept it quiet because who the fuck needs to know?

I feel bad for not telling Melody, but she figured it out anyway because, when I'm around Rhys, I can't fucking hide it.

It's been nice. I don't ask him any questions. I don't touch him. We just fuck, but lately . . . I don't know. Maybe I want a little more.

Maybe I want to know if he's fucking other chicks on the side.

I haven't been with anyone else for a while now. But I don't ask. That would make me vulnerable, and I don't think he'd answer me anyway.

He doesn't talk.

He doesn't want me that way. I'm a warm body for him to sink into.

But after we're done fucking, I have this lingering desire to stay behind, to make him talk to me, to find out who he is. To ask him about his scars on the outside as well as inside.

I made the mistake last night of asking him to tell me about his childhood. Anything. Some stupid little detail about him.

His response?

"Don't." One word. A command. Don't ask.

Because I'm no one to him. And I'm an idiot.

So now, at Quinn's show, I find a warm body to dance with. A body that will fucking dance with me. I turn around, and the guy presses against my ass. I can feel all of him as my eyes lock with Rhys. He's sober. He shouldn't even be in a club, but for his precious Quinn he will be.

I'm starting to figure him out even if he won't talk to me. The way he looks at her? Yeah. She's the one he wants, but she's with Logan now. Quinn told me she used to date Rhys. She played it down like it was nothing, but I can see it meant something to him.

I wonder if he let her touch him. *Did she get to kiss him?*

I bite my bottom lip and make a big show of moaning and leaning back into the nobody behind me. The guy's hands move up my sides as he presses his dick against me, his hands making contact with the rose tattoo Rhys gave me over the fabric of my dress.

I see Rhys's eyes flash with something as they dart to where the guy's hand is touching me.

Does he care?

One of the guy's hands moves over my stomach and pushes up between my breasts as I dance and I allow it, keeping my eyes on Rhys.

I see his jaw ticking with something that looks like jealousy, but I'm not sure if he feels that emotion. I don't know if he feels anything.

The guy's lips move to my neck, and he starts to lick and suck like a slobbery dog. I don't want him to. I don't like it, but still I moan, making sure Rhys thinks this is what I want. Because fuck him.

It's been almost a year of him using my body. Of me accommodating him and letting him fuck me in positions so he doesn't have to look me in the eye. I don't make him talk. I don't make him do anything, and he's all too happy to use me, but he doesn't want to know me. He doesn't want me to know him.

He's like every other guy I've ever known. I thought he was different, but he's not. Soon, he'll be bored. Maybe he already is. And he'll toss me to the side.

He'll find a new toy.

The guy's mouth hurts and not in the good way as he hoovers my neck, leaving his drool behind. "Let's get out of here."

I feel Rhys's eyes on me.

Will he come for me? Stop this guy from escorting me out to fuck me in the bathroom or the alley?

I take the guy's hand and lead him toward the door.

Of course, he won't. And as I push the door open, this guy's hand in mine, no one follows.

No one else even cares.

Rhys

I'VE BEEN HERE A MONTH, and my shop is up and running. It still needs a little work, but with me doing all the work by myself for the last month, it's not bad.

The "OPEN" sign is on, and I've had a decent number of customers already.

Sean has called several times to check on me, and so has Chris. I tell them I'm fine, and that's really all I offer. Because that's just me.

I hate fucking talking.

I think about the night at the shitty club in Chicago that all but ended the good thing I had with Blair. She'd asked me about my childhood, and then, when I didn't fucking tell her, she threw a hissy fit.

She tried her best to make me jealous by dancing with some hipster douchebag and taking him out of the club. She let him touch her in front of me. She touched him to show me she fucking could. That normal guys don't flinch when a hot chick touches them.

That was the worst trip of my life. Being stuck with a vengeful Blair. I mean, what the fuck did she expect? After a year of not letting her touch me, of not talking, that I would all of the sudden open up to her?

Rehab couldn't make me talk about my past. There was no fucking way Badass Barbie was going to make me do it.

The bell on the door dings, and I look up. I'm shocked when a girl around ten- or eleven-years-old with a head-full of wild curls runs in and jumps behind the counter where I'm standing at the front of the shop. dark blue eyes look up at me and pleads, "Hide me."

"What?" I look down at her. She looks lost and afraid. Her clothes look like she goes to a prep school of sorts. Her shoes are nice, no scuffs. But still, I recognize something about her.

I nod at her and look up in time for the bell to ding again and a man in a suit and tie to push through. "Did a little girl come in here?"

I shake my head instantly, feeling the girl crouched at my feet. "No kids allowed."

I point to the sign that says "18 and up." His eyes shift around the shop, searching, and I don't know if it's the suit or something else, but I want to punch the motherfucker in his face for looking around.

"You sure?"

I just glare at him, folding my arms over my wide chest, daring him to ask me again.

He doesn't. He just mumbles something as he leaves. When he's gone, I move to the front and lock the door, changing the sign to "CLOSED" before moving back to behind the counter, seeing the girl on the floor. Her knees are pulled to her chest, and her arms are wrapped around them.

"Please don't make me go back with him."

Fuck! My chest hurts with how hard my heart is pumping. My ears feel like they're going to explode from the pressure as I lean down. "Is he your father?"

Her head shakes from side to side as she lifts her gaze to mine. "Foster father."

I might actually puke. The way she looks. So tiny and afraid. Fuck.

I stand up, fighting to breathe.

I can't fucking breathe.

She's staring up at me, horrified. I'm scaring her.

I force my lungs to cooperate and suck in a big breath before letting it go and crouching down again. "What did he do?"

She looks down at the floor.

No.

"He hurts me."

I want to kill him. I feel my hands form fists involuntarily, and my breaths become rapid, but I remind myself to slow down my breathing. I don't want to scare her. "I won't make you go with him."

She looks up at me with big, hopeful eyes that gut me.

I know why this kid looks so fucking familiar to me now. I don't know what brought her here to my shop, but fuck, maybe we're kindred spirits or something. I can't explain it, but I know I'm supposed to help this kid.

I'll be damned if I let that fucker ever touch her again.

"What's your name?"

"Bree."

I nod my head, liking that she doesn't ask me mine. I haven't earned her trust yet. Good girl. "I'm Rhys."

She just gives me a curt nod because she's a tough kid. Taken in by a sick, twisted rich motherfucker who dresses her up like a doll.

"How old are you?"

"Eleven."

I fight the bile trying to rise in my throat. I can't puke in front of her. That won't inspire any confidence.

"Okay, Bree. I gotta make a call, but the door is locked. Just stay here."

She doesn't move, and I go to the back to grab my cell phone and dial the only person I think I can remotely trust right now. Logan's stepmom. She's a social worker in Kansas City, and even though I'd rather cut off my arm than talk to another social worker again, she's pretty decent.

"Hello?"

"Gillian, it's Rhys."

There's a beat. I wonder if she'll even talk to me. Quinn is her stepson's girl, and when she first moved in with Logan's parents, it was after I had fucking hit Quinn after a bender. My stomach aches, thinking about that. I hit her. I did so many shitty things when I was high.

"Hi, Rhys. Are you okay, sweetie?"

I flinch, not liking any term of endearment. "I'm fine, but a kid just came into my shop. She ran from her foster father, and she told me he hurts her." I swallow the sickening feeling and press forward matter-of-factly. I don't want her to read me. "I can't give her back to that sick motherfucker."

She takes all the information in. "Okay. I'll give you a contact for St. Louis. If she has bruises or any proof."

She won't. Not anywhere they can see, and she won't let them dig too deep. Because she's fucking terrified. "This contact, they're legit?"

"Of course." She thinks they are. I know the system. I've been fucked many times by the system.

"And if she doesn't have any visible bruises?"

She's quiet. "If she's afraid and tells them that, they'll investigate."

I lean my back against the wall, the phone pressed against my ear. "She's scared."

"It will be okay, Rhys. You're doing the right thing. You need to take her to Family Services there and ask for Morgan Winters. She'll help."

I nod and then hang up, walking back to the girl. Bree.

"I'm going to help you."

She looks frightened and so very alone. "You're gonna take me to the social workers." She says it like she already knew what I'd do. Because a kid in the system knows it better than anyone else.

"Yeah."

She stands up, her shoulders drooped. "They'll just put me back in his house."

"I won't let them."

Her head moves from side to side sadly. "He has money." Her

head lifts, and she looks at me, her gaze so fucking heartbreaking I want to punch a hole through the wall. "A lot of it."

My stomach wretches, but I don't let myself throw up. "Let's go. I'll protect you."

And I mean it even if I have no idea how I can do that.

I drive her to Family Services, and we walk inside. The way she walks slowly at my side, it's like I'm guiding her to her slaughter. I fucking hate every step.

We go into the main office, and I holler, "Is there a Morgan Winters here?"

Not too much later, a woman in her forties comes to our aid. "I'm Morgan. Are you Rhys?"

So Gillian called ahead. "Yes."

She smiles warmly, like they're trained to do, as she looks down at Bree. "And you are?"

"Bree."

Morgan nods her head, still with that friendly smile. "Is that your full name?"

The girl huffs, probably having been through it all before. Looking much older than her mere eleven years. Because kids like us grow up fast. "Aubrey Lynn Prescott."

Morgan looks pleased, nodding in approval. "That's great. What a pretty name. And your foster father's name?"

"Mr. Herrington."

Morgan has a little notepad she's scribbling on, nodding her head faster now. "Great. And is he married?"

Bree nods her head. "Yes."

"Okay, that's wonderful. Let me go and do a little bit of research, you guys are welcome to wait for me in the waiting area over there." She points to a line of chairs next to a rack of magazines.

The setup is one I'm painfully familiar with. I lead Bree there, and we sit for all of ten minutes before Morgan summons me to her, leaving Bree to sit and flip through magazines.

"So, who are you to Ms. Prescott?"

"No one. She just ran into my tattoo shop, asking for my help."

She looks over at Bree and then back at me, and I don't like where this is headed already. "Aubrey was placed with the Herringtons a few months ago. They are an upstanding family. Their income is high above the requirements. The mother stays at home. They have two young children. They are more than capable of being her foster parents. They've been doing this for about five years, and there have been zero complaints."

My eyes move to Bree sitting there all alone, her head down, and then I turn back to Morgan, my teeth gritted. "So money. They have money, and they can do whatever they want to that kid."

She looks horrified. "No, of course not, but there have been no complaints."

"So he makes sure they're nice and afraid of him. It's not really hard to do with kids that have nothing."

"And how do you know that?" She's looking at me like I'm the predator. Because I'm rough around the edges in jeans and a t-shirt with tattoos. It's a lot easier to see me that way than the man in the expensive suit.

"Because I lived it."

She studies me and then sighs. "We will look into it."

"Bullshit."

There's that scared look again. "Excuse me?"

"You heard me. You have, what, a hundred kids you look after?" She doesn't argue. I know the system is flooded, especially in the big cities. "She's one. Your investigations are bullshit."

She swallows, and I watch her throat as she gulps with fear. "We'll investigate this. If she's scared, we won't make her go back with him yet."

"Yet." I look back over at Bree, who is looking up now, meeting my eyes in a silent prayer. I turn back to Morgan. "She can stay with me."

"What?" She looks shocked.

"She can stay with me until you can find her somewhere safe."

She shakes her head adamantly. "No. It doesn't work like that, and if you've been in the system before, you know that."

"Oh yeah, I know." It's almost a growl. "What do I need to do? File some paperwork?"

"Yes, you would most certainly need to file paperwork and prove employment." I can see the way she's looking at me. She doesn't believe I have any employment.

"I own my own business." Not a lie, although with Chris fronting the bill, it doesn't feel like the truth either.

"That's impressive." And she clearly didn't expect it. Gillian might trust her, but I don't. I can feel the judgment. "How old are you?"

"My age matters?"

"Yes." She nods without hesitation.

"Twenty-three."

Her lips form a thin line, and I know it seems too young, even though I feel forty. "I see. Are you married?"

"What does that have to do with anything?"

She acts like she's trying with me but I'm on her last nerve. "Listen, you're a young, single man wanting a young unrelated female to move in with you. Do you know how that sounds?"

"I would never fucking touch her." I'm struggling to stay calm. Even the subtle hint that I might be interested in her for anything other than to protect her makes me sick to my stomach.

"But we can't place her with you. You have to understand that, right?"

"Just give me the fucking paperwork. I'll do the rest."

She huffs and searches through her desk. "It will take days to process, or weeks." I look over at Bree, knowing she doesn't have weeks. She hands me papers, and I grasp them tightly in my hands. "She'll have to stay in an approved temporary home."

"But not with that fucker?"

She flinches at my language. You'd think she'd be used to it by now, working with foster kids and all. "No. If she's afraid of him, we will investigate."

I only have a couple of days. I know it by the way she's talking. She wants to get Bree back into the so-called "good home." The one she feels is one of her easy cases in a clean, upstanding neighborhood.

"I'll be back."

She nods her head solemnly as I walk away from her and explain the situation to Bree. The kid doesn't cry. We don't cry. We don't show weakness.

"I'll be back for you, Bree."

She doesn't believe me. I get it.

I leave her with my promise, but I know it means nothing until the action is there.

As I walk out of the building, my heart is racing for a whole new reason because I know who I have to go to for help.

And she doesn't owe me anything because I've never given her anything.

Rhys

About a year ago

W E'RE FINALLY BACK from that godawful trip, and I wish I could just not think about Blair. That would be great, but I can't stop.

My body wants a release.

And I swear, she's the only one who can give it to me at this point.

I show up at her house, hoping Melody isn't here.

Blair answers the door, looking shocked that I'm here, and all I can see is that fucker grinding on her at the bar.

The hickeys on her neck the next day.

"What the fuck do you want?"

I stand there and stare at her, and she walks out of her house.

"Oh, that's right. You don't answer questions."

She's that fucking pissed-off that I won't talk about my childhood? Seriously?

"Did you fuck him?"

She scoffs, tossing her hair over her shoulder and acting like I'm ridiculous. "And if I did? What the hell do you care, Rhys?"

What do I care? I don't own her. I barely even like her. But seeing that fucker's hands all over her did something to me I don't understand.

I wanted to break his face and toss her over my shoulder, dragging her ass out of the bar.

"I don't."

"Exactly." She lifts a finger in the air, pointing at me. "You don't care. So why are you at my house, huh? You want me to strip for you?" She's spitting venom. "You want me to press up against the wall and let you pound into me? Your own personal little fuck doll?"

I bare my teeth. "And what do you care? Isn't that what we've always done?"

She's seething with rage. She looks like she wants to hit me. "Not anymore. You can't give me any fucking thing back, then no. You can't use my body anymore."

Give her anything back? What the hell does she want from me? I scoff, and it's cruel. "So why the fucking change because you didn't seem to mind me using your body until before the trip. Never expected something from me."

She swallows, and if I didn't know better, I'd say she had tears in her eyes. "Because I won't be tossed away like trash." She turns and walks away from me, but I hear, "not by you," under her breath before she walks inside her house.

I have no idea what the fuck just happened.

I should be the one who is mad, if anyone is. She fucked some other guy on a trip with me. Well, a trip with Melody, Sean, and me.

But still.

What the fuck?

I can't give her anything, but that was always part of the deal she knew about, right?

Rhys

As soon as I left Family Services, I called Gillian and told her everything. While she sounded sympathetic, I didn't end the call too hopeful. I know I sound like a crazy person. That on the surface, Bree's foster parents seem great. But I saw her face. I know something is very, very wrong.

She's going to do her best to pull some strings in the system, and I'm going to do my best to make myself look good on paper.

Because I can't let that girl I just met down. I can't.

I park my car and walk up to Ashton Inc.'s St. Louis office, looking for the one person who can help me.

And lucky for me, she's walking down the stairs before I even make it there. She looks horrified when she sees me. "Rhys?"

I nod dumbly. "I need your help."

She does exactly what I expect. She laughs, brushing past me. "You drove a long way for me to tell you to fuck off."

"So, then don't." I follow behind her as she starts toward the parking lot and stop when she spins around to face me.

"What could you possibly want? It really wasn't that long ago that I let you fuck me in a bathroom stall."

I ignore that, knowing she's trying to bait me. Blair likes to push buttons. She wants the challenge, but I don't have time for that. "Move in with me."

Blair is rarely shocked, but her jaw is almost touching the sidewalk. "What?"

"I need you to move in with me. I need a steady, live-in girlfriend."

"Are you high?" She takes a step closer to me but doesn't touch me. She's always respected that. "You have to be."

"I'm sober." I know I sound insane. "Blair, I need your help."

"You want me to move in with you? Leave my job and my new house and just move back to Kansas City with you?"

I reach around the back of my neck, gripping it with my hand, knowing she's going to be really pissed now. "I, uh . . . actually live here now."

"What?" *Yup. Pissed.* "What the fuck are you talking about? Here where?"

"Downtown St. Louis. Chris gave me my own shop here, and I live above it."

I expect her to give me shit about my long sentence, but she doesn't. She's just plain furious because she's smart and connected the dots. "You knew you were moving here when we fucked in the bathroom and I told you I was moving to St. Louis?"

I nod because she already knows the truth. I look guilty as fuck. "Yes."

"Why didn't you tell me then?" She doesn't let me answer and throws her arms up in the air. "Of course, you didn't fucking tell me. Because that would be offering information about yourself, letting me in slightly. And you don't fucking do that."

"And I've never hidden that fact about myself."

Her eyes roll, and I'm glad she folds her arms over her chest because she looks like she wants to claw my eyes out. "No, you haven't. I'm just a fucking idiot."

"I have no idea what you're talking about."

She laughs, but it's cold. "Why the fuck do you want me to move in with you here? Are you lonely, Rhys?"

It's a cold mocking tone. "No. I need your help with a little girl."

Her eyes narrow, and I see the curiosity under the fury. "A little girl."

"An eleven-year-old foster girl. I need to get her out of the home she's in."

"How long have you been here?"

"A month," I answer quickly. No point in lying and again, no fucking time. I need to get all of this moving.

"And you've already met an eleven-year-old girl who needs your help, and you want to what? Adopt her?"

"No." I shake my head, dropping my hand from my neck. "I don't know. I just need to be a temporary place for her to stay until they can get her into a good place. And I can't do that as a single man."

"So you want me to play house with you to help get you a little girl?"

I groan, "Please don't say it like that. That's fucking creepy."

"Yeah. It is." She waves her hands, dismissing me and starts toward the parking lot again. "Find someone else. I'm sure you can get some dumbass girl to pretend to love you."

I follow her across the street to the parking lot and run in front of her to make her stop. "I can't do this with a stranger, Blair. I need your help." I hate asking for help. The words taste bad in my mouth. But there's no way I could do this with anyone else. Even if she's mad at me, Blair gets me on some level. She knows I'm fucked-up.

"You might as well be a stranger to me, Rhys."

I stare at her, unsure what she wants from me. "You never wanted me to talk before. You never asked questions." I liked that about her.

She folds her arms over her chest, just staring at me.

Is it answers she wants? Because I don't know if I can do that.

Blair

THIS HAS to be a fucking joke, right?

He wants me to move in with him so he can get custody of some kid. *He fucking lives here in St. Louis. And has for the same month that I have.* "Do you know this kid?"

"I just met her."

His short answers make me homicidal. "Yeah, well. Good luck with that, Rhys."

I move past him, still careful not to make contact even though I'm pissed-off. He's still following me, and when we reach my car, I make a huge mistake and turn around to look at him.

God. Damn. It.

"Explain." I fold my arms over my chest, staring at him with fury because I want to kill him. He didn't fucking tell me he was moving. Because he doesn't give a damn about me.

"A kid came into my shop yesterday. Scared." He shakes his head. "No. Fucking terrified. She told me her foster father hurts her. She asked me to hide her."

"Why would she go to you?"

He seems so lost. Out of control. And it's awful to see. "I have no idea. None. But she did. For whatever reason, she flew into my shop yesterday, and she needs my help. They aren't going to give her to some strange guy who she's not related to. But they *will* give her to some strange couple she's not related to. You know Logan's stepmom?"

"Gillian." I've only met her a few times, but she seems nice enough.

"She's a social worker. She's going to try to work some magic, but I need to make it as easy as I can. And if I'm not living alone, it'll look a hell of a lot better."

I huff and drop my arms, hating that I'm even giving him the time of day, but he looks so desperate. And Rhys does not ask for help. "How do you know this girl is really in trouble?"

His gaze is hard. His eyes almost black. "Because I know."

That's not an answer, but it is a Rhys answer." "How long?"

He looks surprised that I'm even entertaining the idea, and he should be. I'm surprised at myself. "I don't know. It might be a month or two."

A month or two living with Rhys and a strange little girl. "I know nothing about raising a kid. I don't *want* to know anything about raising a kid."

"I'll do it all. It's just for show." He holds up his hands in surrender. "I'll sleep on the couch. I won't touch you."

I nearly snort at the idea. Him not touching me. "I'm not staying in whatever shithole you're living in, and I doubt that it will look that great to social services."

He looks annoyed, but shockingly, he doesn't fight me. "What do you suggest then?"

"You two can move into my house, I guess. It's nice. Big. Enough room for you to stay the fuck away from me and appease social services."

He lets out a long breath of air, almost like he was holding it. "Okay. Thank you."

"You really think that you're what's best for this kid?"

He nods his head once, and he does look certain. "It's better than where she was, Blair."

My name on his lips sends a shudder through me I'm not proud of.

"When do you move in?"

"I'm filing the paperwork tomorrow morning. Gillian is doing her best to put everything through fast. If all goes well, by Friday."

I swallow my nerves, determined not to let him see.

"Fine. My number's still the same. Call me when you have the details."

He nods, and I grab my door handle opening it, not chancing another glance back at him as I climb inside.

What the hell did I just agree to?

Rhys

Gillian is a fucking magician. I have no idea how she did it, but she managed to get us qualified as temporary housing status in the system.

It's not a permanent solution by any means, but it gives me more time. Time to apply to be an actual foster parent for Bree.

I have to file a whole new set of paperwork for that, and it can take a couple of months, but Gillian is going to try to push that through.

I never thought I would grow up to have a connection to a social worker. I grew up despising them all, but I'm grateful for her right now.

I go into the Family Services building and find Morgan, who is clearly not happy with me. I have no idea what her connection to Gillian is, but she's definitely not the bright and shiny type. She's glaring daggers at me as she questions me again, going over the paperwork.

"You live with a Blair Ashton?"

I nod my head and point to the paper. "Yes. At that address. We just moved here."

She's not buying it, and she has definitely dropped the Mary Poppins routine now that Bree isn't standing right here. I'm glad she did. It was annoying. "How long have you been dating?"

Again, I point to the paper. "Three years." I mean, that's how long I've been fucking her.

"Any plans to marry?"

I almost gulp at the questions. Marriage has never crossed my mind. Ever. "Does that matter?"

She peers up at me over the rims of her glasses that have slid down her nose. "Yes. Are you committed to this woman?"

I don't lie to the people in my life. The people I care about. But to people in this system, fuck yeah, I'll lie. "Yes."

She huffs and looks down at the paper. "You were in rehab?"

Fuck, woman. I thought Gillian had it handled, but it sure feels like an interrogation. "I was. I've been clean for five years."

"And you're only twenty-three."

My patience is wearing thin. "What exactly is your problem with me? My tattoos? My past? The fact that I don't have much money? Or just all of it?"

This is why I'm quiet most of the time. I have zero tolerance for humans. She looks up at me, removing her glasses. "Do you know how many children I see every single day. Children who would kill to be in a home with the Herringtons?"

There's that vomit feeling again. Because I know she's right. "Just because something looks shiny on the outside doesn't mean it's good."

"Nothing tells me that they are bad."

"Except for Bree."

She shakes her head at me as if I'm naïve. I'm not. "Bree is no angel." I feel my fists clenching against my thighs. "She's been disruptive in school. She's been caught lying and stealing. She's eleven, but she has quite the record. And Mr. And Mrs. Herrington were overlooking all of that. They wanted to adopt her, but because you got involved that whole process has been put on hold, and you don't even know this girl."

That fucker will never adopt her. "And neither do you. And so fucking what if she acts out? Maybe she was screaming for help."

"This was long before the Herringtons, Mr. Moore. What if they were the answer to her prayers?"

"What if they were her nightmare?" I sit still, but my skin is crawling, itching for relief. I'm wound tight, and what I really need is a meeting, but I stay in my seat.

Again, she shakes her head at me. "Do you know the things they could have given her? The education? The clothes? The social status? And to be honest with you, they still might if I have my way."

I stare into her eyes, unwavering. "You'll have to go through me, and I may seem like a nobody, but I can be your worst nightmare."

Her glare doesn't even begin to penetrate me. I've been up against far worse. "You realize I'm going to be up your ass? You mess up one time, and it's over. I don't care who you know."

"And yet, you're only just now investigating the Herringtons and will probably do a piss poor job at it."

"You should probably start regarding me with a little respect, Mr. Moore."

I stand, towering over her. "Respect is tough to earn and easily lost. I have no idea why you have Gillian's respect, and I don't care. But you don't have mine. I'll jump through the hoops though. Where's Bree?"

She sucks in a deep breath and stands. "She's in the office. I'll go get her and her things. I will be by for a surprise inspection very soon."

I can hear the threat in her words, and I know I have a lot to do today. It wouldn't surprise me if she showed up tomorrow. "Not a problem."

"You're robbing this girl. You understand that? You may have never gotten a break, but this is hers."

I don't say anything. Just stand still, staring at her until she moves away from me, retreating and then bringing Bree back. She doesn't look thrilled, but I'm pretty sure that's just her face. Another thing we have in common.

"You ready?"

She nods, slinging her little duffle bag over her shoulder, and I quickly take it, putting it on my own shoulder. She doesn't argue with me, but I feel like she wants to.

She's watching Morgan with hesitance as the woman bends down in front of her to get to eye level. "If you need anything at all, please call me. Okay?" Morgan's eyes meet mine and then back to Bree. "Anything at all."

Bree shrugs her off, not falling for the nice act in the slightest. That's the thing about street kids, we can read people better than anyone else on the planet.

"I'm fine."

I like the hint of attitude and lead her out of this hell hole without another glance to Ms. Winters.

We reach my car before Bree says anything. "So how long am I staying with you?"

It's not hopeful. Or even really the curiosity of a kid. It's just what it is. A blank question, knowing the system is out to fuck her over.

"I have shit to work out, but if I have anything to say about it, you'll be with me until I can find you somewhere truly safe."

Her little brow crinkles, her hair still down with curls everywhere. "Does that place exist?"

I'm not sure, but I'm going to try to find it if it does.

Blair

OH MY GOD, *what the hell did I agree to?* I'm really not sure I can do this, but I guess I'm going to. Rhys sent a text that they're on their way about an hour ago, and I left work early so I'd be here.

It's all happening fast.

The doorbell rings, and when I open the door, there's Rhys in all his broody, silent fucking hot glory. He didn't dress up for social services. He's wearing jeans and a black t-shirt that would make any straight woman fucking drool.

I look down at the girl at his side. She's a skinny, bony little thing. Pretty face. Almost like a doll, but her hair is unruly as all hell. The brown curls are everywhere, and I wonder if she brushed them this morning. She's wearing a little plaid jumper with a white shirt, but it seems wrong.

I don't think it's her style at all.

"Blair."

"Hey, Rhys."

The girl looks from me to him and then back at me. Then back to him, pointing up at me. "This is your girlfriend?"

Rhys looks uncomfortable, but we agreed it would be best to keep her in the dark about what we actually are in order to protect her from having to lie. "Yes."

"Hi, I'm Blair."

Her blue eyes flash to mine, and she seems almost annoyed. She looks back at Rhys. "Really?"

I swear, Rhys almost cracks an honest-to-God smile as if these two have some kind of inside joke. "Yes. Really." He turns to me. "Can we come in?"

I nod and move out of the way as he walks in, carrying two bags.

I'm still trying here even though I have no idea how to be nice. She's a kid though. How hard can it be. "So you're Bree."

It's not a question, but she rolls her eyes at me. "Good job." She looks over at Rhys again, angling her thumb in my direction. "I didn't think you'd be with a Barbie."

I glare at Rhys, and his eyes widen slightly, probably realizing I'm not above slapping an eleven-year-old as he steps in between us, looking at her. "She's Badass Barbie, if it helps."

Again, the kid rolls her eyes, and I'm about to throttle Rhys. Really? He had to choose this one?

He turns to look at me, a pleading look on his face. "Sorry."

"Did she seriously just call me a fucking Barbie?"

"Have you looked in a mirror, lately?" The little brat has some fucking nerve.

Rhys holds up a hand in my direction. "Blair, you're the one that called yourself a fucking Barbie when we first met."

"I don't like it," I growl.

He just shrugs. "So, put on fifty pounds. Take out the tits. Let me tattoo your face."

I place one hand on my hip and glare at him. "Are you seriously going to give me shit right now? After everythi—"

He moves to stand right in front of me, and honestly, I don't think we've ever been this close, face-to-face. At least not for a long, long time. He looks desperate, and there's something not quite right in his eyes. "No. I'm not. I swear. I'm sorry."

I huff and drop my hand from my hip. "Fine. Whatever." I look over at Bree. "Do you want to see your room?"

She just shrugs. "Sure."

Oh great. There's two of them.

I lead the way, and they both follow, not saying a word. I wonder if they talked at all in the car. Are either of them capable of it?

I lead them up the stairs, past my office and to the next bedroom on the left, pushing open the door. "Okay. This is your room. I didn't have much time to prepare, but I figured we can go shopping to add some touches to your room. I had no idea what you would be into. Clearly not Barbies."

She scrunches her nose at that and looks around the plain room. There's a full bed that still has some boring adult bedding on it. Solid purple. There's a dresser, and the bathroom is shared with the office, but it will just be hers. I bought her some shampoo and toiletries that I left on the sink.

"This is fine." She sits on the bed. "It's only temporary, right?"

It's not a real question, and the kid doesn't seem to have much hope. Maybe Rhys was right. She doesn't seem like an eleven-year-old, not that I've been around any since I was eleven.

Still, she lacks childhood innocence.

"Well, we can still go get you some stuff, and you can take it with you if you leave."

Again, her little brow furrows, and she looks annoyed before she shrugs. Rhys just looks fucking uncomfortable.

But that's Rhys.

"Okay. Well, I'll let you settle in."

She nods, and I exit, feeling Rhys follow. I hate how I know his scent. I dream about that scent sometimes, manly and safe. Even though I've never been able to lay my head on his shoulder or really have long enough to really take him all in, I know how he smells. And it's fucking delicious.

"You don't really have to stay on the couch."

He shrugs. "I don't mind."

"Won't that be suspicious if the social worker comes to check on us?"

His eyes darken, and I wonder what happened at the meeting. He looks around the second floor. "Does this place have another room?"

It does.

Still, I find myself wanting him in my bed. "Another room would be the same thing as the couch."

His eyes meet mine. "Blair. I can't sleep in the same bed with you."

I think I'm actually blushing with embarrassment from being so fucking stupid. "Of course not."

I start to walk away, needing some space, but his hand catches mine. I look up at him in shock, and he lets go like I bit him. "I can't sleep with anyone, Blair."

I nod, feeling that familiar soft spot I have for him. "My bedroom is huge." I gesture for him to follow me down the hall where my bedroom is located. I push through the double doors of the massive room to show him I'm not kidding.

He looks around, his eyes taking in every detail, but I swear the way he's looking at it, it might as well be a prison. I have a king-sized bed, and a large flat screen. There are two comfy chairs and a pink chaise lounge chair by the window. I point at it. "You could sleep there, but I think you're longer than it is."

He nods his head. "Okay."

I look at him like he's crazy because clearly he is. "Rhys, I was kidding."

"I'm not." His eyes tell me he's deadly serious. "It's fine. I've slept in way worse."

I flop down on my bed, my arm flung over my eyes as my head is angled up at the ceiling. My feet are still on the floor. "What if we put pillows between us? It seems really fucking stupid to have you sleep on that thing."

Just because he's afraid we might what? End up spooning in the middle of the night.

"The chair is fine."

I sit up and look over at him. "Fine. Have it your way. I'm gonna take the little brat shopping."

"Don't call her that." He doesn't seem irritated though, almost like he finds the nickname amusing.

"She's awful, Rhys. You know that, right?" My eyes meet his, and my tone is playful even though I hate it because I actually like her already. Even if she called me "Barbie" and gave me a ton of attitude. She's obviously hellbent on giving me a hard time.

"Yeah, but she's kind of great."

I smile. "Aw, you're smitten."

He rolls his eyes. "I've never been smitten. She's a tough kid. And you do look like a Barbie."

I meet his eyes, my hands itching to touch him, but I don't. "Then you must have a Barbie fantasy."

He doesn't argue. "Thank you, Blair."

I don't know how to handle how he's looking at me. "It's not really that big of a deal. The house is huge."

"I'm going to go check on her."

I nod dumbly as he leaves, and I watch him walking up the stairs.

I could be in over my head here.

Rhys

BLAIR IS TRULY AMAZING. There's no denying it.

I know I'm hard to deal with, and Bree hasn't taken to Blair yet, so she's not going to make it easy.

Still, Blair had her room ready. She was willing to share her bed with me. And not only that, she took Bree to the store, and they came back with a ton of shit.

Bree didn't look thrilled, and I'm sure that's confusing to Blair, but I know she was grateful even if she doesn't trust Blair yet.

"Hopefully she sleeps okay."

Blair sits on the step next to me on the front porch of her house. She leaves several inches between our thighs. "She will. That bed looks nice."

"Better than a fucking chair."

I know she's irritated with me. I've never slept in a bed with anyone else before. It's not personal. It's dark out, but the street she lives on is well lit with streetlights and porch lights. Sedans drive by every once and awhile, probably fathers coming home to their kids.

"Thanks for today."

She lifts her shoulders, her breasts lifting as she takes in a deep breath and then falling when she releases it. "It's nothing." She stretches her legs out in front of her. She's wearing a black leather skirt so her legs are on full display. They're smooth with just enough muscle from her morning runs. "But what is the plan exactly?"

I shrug because I have no fucking idea. "Keep her safe."

"Right . . ." I feel her eyes on the side of my face as I look everywhere but at her. "Don't freak out on me."

I turn suddenly at that, and she holds her hands up, "I'm not going to touch you. Chill."

"What?" I would love to say that wasn't my first thought, but it was. "Why would I freak out?"

"How do you know she wasn't safe?"

My teeth grind in my mouth, and I hate how she sounds dangerously close to the social worker bitch. "She wasn't."

"Rhys, don't get so defensive. I want to know." Her voice has an edge to it like she's annoyed, but I also hear the softness there. She deserves some sort of explanation since she's offering up her house.

"She told me she wasn't."

She's gnawing on her bottom lip, and it's actually funny to me that I can make her nervous. "People lie, Rhys. Even little girls."

"That's what's fucked with the system." My eyes meet hers, and I try not to sound so harsh. "They believe that kids will lie, but they don't realize adults are far more likely to be corrupt."

She thinks that over. "I guess that makes sense. Every adult I know is a total twat."

I actually laugh at that. In my own way. It's probably more of a scoff. "Exactly."

"Rhys Moore, did you just laugh?"

I shrug my shoulders and clear my throat. "No."

She scoffs, shaking her head. "Right."

I know I owe her more than this. "I was a foster kid, Blair."

She tilts her head to look at me as if to say no shit. "I know that. I pay a little attention, Rhys."

I swallow the sickening feeling, trying to ignore my sweaty palms and rapid heart rate. "I was in a lot of bad homes." My throat is dry as I try my best to swallow the lump there. "But the last one was the worst by far."

She doesn't ask me what happened. And I'm grateful, but still I owe her something.

"There was abuse. And I just know this girl has felt that. I don't know how to explain it . . . I just . . ."

"Feel it," she supplies, her voice quiet and almost breathless.

"Yes."

"Okay. So, we protect her." She says it with determination like it's the easiest thing in the world. And when I look at her pretty face, I want so fucking badly to taste her lips, but I fucking can't.

Because I'm so fucking broken and fucked-up that the thought also makes me sweat with fear.

Tremble even.

"Will you be okay here with her if I go to the gym?"

She nods her head, leaning back on the step, letting her elbows rest on the porch behind her. "Yes, but there's equipment here."

"You have a home gym?"

Her eyes roll. "Of course. It's in the basement."

"I'll go to my own. Thanks." I stand up and look back at her. "Yours probably only has girly shit.'"

She stands up, facing me as she flips me off. "It's state of the art, fucker."

I don't want to get too familiar with her home or take even more advantage than I already have. "I'll be back in an hour."

I need to let off some steam before I lose my shit.

"Rhys?"

"Yeah?"

"What are the rules?"

I stare at her, uncertain about what she's asking. "Rules?"

"Yeah. I mean . . . you aren't going to touch me, and I'm not even close to dried up."

I cringe at her description. "Nice."

She laughs easily and shrugs. "It's true."

"Oh, I know." She laughs again, responding to my semi-playful side. "You can fuck whoever you want, Blair."

"And the social worker won't care? We're supposed to be in a relationship, right?"

"I don't think she's gonna dig that deep. Maybe don't bring them here."

She thinks it over but seems annoyed with me yet again. "Fine."

I don't stay to talk any longer and walk to my car to drive to the gym across town near my shop.

I hate the idea of other motherfuckers touching her, but at least they can, and she can touch them back without them flinching like a pussy.

Rhys

When I get back from the gym, I think about ringing the doorbell even though Blair gave me a key. It feels like an odd invasion of privacy just walking into her home.

But I go ahead and do it since it's after ten. I doubt she's asleep yet. I showered at the gym, so I head upstairs where I left all my stuff. I suppose it makes sense to sleep in her room, but it still feels too intimate even if her room is bigger than my apartment and I'm sleeping across from her.

I see Bree's light is still on and her door is open, so I knock real quick to check on her.

She's reading on her bed and looks at me funny. "You don't have to knock when I can see you."

I walk in, ignoring the attitude I actually like. If she had no fight left, I would really worry. "You okay? You need anything?"

She shakes her head and points to the several shopping bags that are sitting on the floor under her window. "No. Your Barbie loaded me up."

"She didn't buy you a lot of pink shit, did she?"

She smirks at that and closes her book. "No. She was actually pretty cool. Let me get jeans and t-shirts. A really cool jacket. Some vintage stuff for the room." She shrugs. "It wasn't too bad."

"Yeah, Blair really isn't that bad."

She lifts her little shoulders. "She still looks like a Barbie."

I almost laugh. This kid seems to do that to me. "Yeah. I know. But don't tell her. Makes her all pissy."

She smiles. "Yeah. I know." She looks nervous now as her head dips, her gaze staying away from me and her voice is quiet. "Please don't ask me."

"I won't." I know what she's talking about. I don't want to ask her. "But you can talk to me if you need to. Or Blair. When we earn it."

Her eyes lift slowly. "You think I'll be here long enough for that?"

"If I have anything to say about it, yeah."

But we both know the process. We both know the hoops they're going to make me jump through will be huge. "He wanted me to be this perfect little doll. That's not me."

"You don't have to be anyone's doll." My voice is too harsh to talk to a child, but she doesn't flinch.

"I thought that's what your Barbie was gonna do today. Dress me up the way she wanted me to." I listen quietly. "But she asked me what I liked."

I tense because that's very Blair. "She cares. More than most, even if she doesn't seem like it at first."

She nods her head at that, thinking it over.

"You sure you don't need anything?"

She nods, shooing me away.

"School tomorrow. Go to bed soon, okay?"

She dismisses me again, and I leave her to it, walking down the hall to the double doors down at the end. They're open, and Blair is sitting on her bed as well, flipping through channels on her TV.

She turns when she sees me. She's wearing the world's shortest pink shorts and a cropped, matching camisole. I've seen her naked, but this isn't much different. "Fuck, Blair. You think you could find some real pajamas?"

She rolls her eyes, flipping me off and turning the television off. "You're lucky I'm wearing anything. I usually sleep completely naked."

And now my mind is exactly where she wanted it. Her naked body.

"I can sleep on the couch. I don't want to put you out."

She waves me off. "Or you could not be a pussy and sleep in the bed."

She's in a mood, but when isn't she? I ignore her and take my shoes and socks off, worn out from the gym. "Her school isn't far. I'll drop her off on my way to work."

"I don't mind taking her."

I look over at her as I remove my shirt and drop it next to the chair I'm sleeping on. "She grow on you?"

She scoffs, but I think she did. "She's feisty. I like it."

"Yeah. Me too." I reach for my bag and find a pair of sweats. I should change in the bathroom, especially since Blair's eyes haven't stayed off my chest since I took off my shirt. "You're like a dude, you know?"

She laughs at that and pulls her covers back. "You have a nice body. I'm supposed to ignore it?"

I guess I stare at her tits often enough. "You could try."

She rolls her eyes and slides under the covers. "If you don't want me looking, maybe you should skip the gym. Don't tell me you do all that working out just for fun."

I don't. But the way I stiffen when she says that, I think she knows there's a more sinister reason I work out as much as I do. And I don't like it. I push my shorts down and off and quickly pull the sweats on.

She doesn't question me, just gets situated on her bed as I lay down on the soft chair, pulling the blanket she left for me over my body. She tells the device in her room to turn off the lights, and we're left in the dark.

"Ask me."

I barely recognize my voice. The two words coming out shaky.

"Ask you what, Rhys?"

"One question. Whatever you want to." I know I owe her more

than the shitty explanation I gave her earlier. She made Bree feel comfortable here. She let us move in and rearrange her life.

"What's the point? You won't answer it anyway."

"I wouldn't offer if I didn't plan to answer. Go ahead. One."

My hands shake at my side as I hope she doesn't ask the truly difficult questions, but I'll answer whatever she asks me.

She's quiet for what seems like an eternity and then finally softly asks, "How old were you when you went into foster care?"

Damn, she went easy on me. I take a deep breath. Thankful for that.

"Three. My mom dropped me at one of those Safe Drop places."

"Jesus," she whispers into the darkness. I think if she reacts that way to the easy question, she better not ask any tough ones. "What a twat."

That word sounds funny coming out of her mouth. I have no idea why it gets me, but it does, and I half-laugh again.

"I know that was a fucking laugh this time."

I smile in the dark room and settle into the pillow. "Maybe."

"Thank you."

"I didn't want you to feel like you were living with a total stranger."

"So, does that mean the longer you're here, the more questions you'll answer?"

I shrug even if she can't see me. "Maybe."

I don't want her to dig deeper. I don't want to talk, but if there's anyone I will answer to, it's Blair.

Rhys

Yeah, that fucking chair sucks ass. I groan and pull my tired body up and off the pink lounge chair in Blair's room.

It's not like I sleep much anyway. And besides, I've slept on much worse. Blair's bed is empty, and I grab a shirt, tugging it on before I walk down the hall. Bree's door is wide open, and she's not inside either.

I walk down the stairs, and the smell of bacon hits my nose first. What the fuck? Blair knows how to cook?

I walk into the kitchen and see a full plate of food in front of Bree, who's sitting at the table. I look at Blair, with an eyebrow lifted because I really didn't expect her to cook. She's still wearing the little shorts and cropped top from last night, but she did put a robe over it. She just didn't tie it.

"Blair?" It's a question as I look over at the table again, seeing Bree eating slowly.

Blair just lifts her shoulders, handing me a mug full of black, hot coffee. "I don't know how to cook, but I definitely know how to order food." She nods toward the brown bag on the counter from a local breakfast place.

That makes more sense. But I don't say that, considering I would like my balls to stay attached to my body, and she's really trying here. "Thanks."

I take a drink of coffee and sit down across from Bree. She doesn't look up from her plate. She's wearing a t-shirt today though, her curls pulled up in a ponytail. This seems more like her style, and I'm grateful to Blair for that.

Not dressing her up like a fucking doll. I can see she has on ripped jeans, ripped for style and not from wear.

"You ready for school?"

She shrugs as she takes a bite of breakfast potatoes. Blair sets a plate in front of me and then takes a seat with some fruit in front of her. Bree scrunches her nose as she shakes her head in disapproval at Blair's breakfast choice. "No wonder you look like a Barbie."

It doesn't bother Blair this time as she pokes a piece of strawberry with her fork and brings it to her mouth. "I hope you're not calling me skinny, string bean."

Bree glowers at her, but I can tell Blair is starting to get in. She goes back to her breakfast, and I take a bite of the eggs on my plate. I tossed and turned all night and not because of the shitty accommodations. I can't get that fucking social worker's words out of my head.

That I'm robbing Bree of a good life. I can't give her any of the things the Herringtons can. I can barely take care of myself. And I can't ask Blair to do this forever.

"I can take you to school, string bean. If you want." I look over at Blair.

"I'll take her."

She takes another bite of fruit. "I don't mind. I just thought I'd offer since it's the opposite direction for you."

Bree, of course, doesn't really express her opinion either way. "Whatever."

"I'll take you today." My nerves are on high alert, and I have an overwhelming need to make sure she's safe.

Not that Blair can't keep her safe.

Bree stands up after finishing most of her breakfast. "I'm gonna go read before school."

I nod, and she leaves as Blair turns to me. "I'm not trying to step on your toes. I really don't mind."

"You've done enough. I told you, she'll be my responsibility."

She looks wounded by my words, and it's beginning to annoy me that she's starting to act like an actual chick and not the Blair I know.

She's studying me, and I don't fucking like it. "Stop."

She rolls her eyes and looks away. "Right. No eye contact. I thought that was just when we were fucking."

I glare at her, my jaw clenched tight, hating how that fucking stung. "Just stop trying to dig deeper. I'm not a deep well, Blair. I'm just a shattered surface."

Her eyes meet mine again. "You should be a poet." She's being sarcastic, of course, as she takes a drink of her coffee. "What the hell is wrong with you?"

"Too fucking much." I stand up from the table, but she does too.

"No, I mean something new is eating at you. You got temporary clearance to be her foster dad. Is it getting approval for longer?"

Yes. And no. I'm starting to think Gillian has some serious pull. "I just don't know if I'm doing the best thing for her."

My teeth are nearly grinding in my mouth. Doubt is a motherfucker, but how can I not doubt this? I'm a street kid from nothing. I don't know how to be a parent. I barely know how to function.

"What's making you second guess this?"

Every fucking thing. But I don't tell her anything. That leads to more talking, and I just want this shut down. "Nothing. I'm fine."

"Oh bullshit. Look, I know you don't like it, but I can read you." She shrugs. "At least better than most. Just tell me because you dragged me into this. You made me your partner, so you have to talk to me."

"Jesus, Blair. Do you ever shut up?"

Most girls would cry. Not Blair. "No, and I won't. I'll hound your ass until you tell me, which is exhausting for both of us. So just fucking tell me."

My hand grips my hair, threatening to pull it out of my head. She gives me a headache. "The social worker is against it. Said I was cheating Bree."

"That bitch."

I drop my hand. "Yeah. But she's right in a way."

"Bree is afraid of that asshole. You aren't cheating her. You're protecting her."

And now it's pretty clear she believes me about Bree needing to be away from that man. "I don't mean she should ever go back to him, but . . ." She's listening too intently, paying attention to my every move. I hate feeling this vulnerable. "I don't know if I'm the better option."

She's letting that sink in, really thinking about it, and every second ticking by is torture. "You are. You've already been more of a father to her than she's probably ever had."

"How? Bringing her to my fake girlfriend's house." She flinches, but quickly recovers.

"By protecting her. Helping her when she asked for help. That's all she needs."

Bree walks in with her backpack slung over her shoulder. "Is one of you going to take me to school?"

I grab my keys from the kitchen counter and nod my head curtly in Blair's direction. The only way I know how to end the conversation I didn't want to have in the first place.

She walks over to Bree, smoothing her hair with her hand. "Give 'em hell, kid. You have my number and your cell."

"She has a cellphone?" I walk to join the girls.

Bree lifts her shoulder in a signature shrug. "Yeah. Blair made me get one."

Blair eyes me with determination that says, don't fight me on this. "She needs to be able to call us."

I nod in agreement. "I could have gotten her a phone."

Blair rolls her eyes, folding her arms right under her full breasts, only pushing them up more and drawing my attention. She smirks when she sees where my gaze is focused. "I got to it first. We're all a team here."

Bree starts for the door. "Whatever, can we go?"

"Thanks," I say to Blair in a forced manner that doesn't bother her as she waves me off.

"No problem."

I take Bree to school and drop her off, handing her backpack to her as she climbs out. "I'll pick you up."

"K." She closes the door and then heads up toward the school. I see two guys around her age in dingy jeans and shirts nod at her as the three of them talk and joke around in front of the public school that looks a lot like the one I went to. It's not really in Blair's district, but Bree was already enrolled here this year.

The boys she's hanging with remind me all too much of me. Rough and tough, already jaded by life at eleven.

But they seem protective of Bree, which I guess is okay with me.

I leave, driving toward my shop, but I can't stop my mind from wandering to everywhere but the shop.

I know Bree would hate a private school, but wouldn't it give her a better shot at life? Isn't that what I should do?

I want to prove that bitch at social services wrong. I want to be the best thing for Bree.

Blair

I GET HOME FROM WORK, and it's almost bizarre to hear people in the house. I know it's Rhys and Bree, but still, it's kind of weird.

Weirdly nice. They're making a mess in the kitchen though.

The stove is on, and I can see water boiling as Rhys and Bree gather around his phone, looking at it intently.

"What's up?"

They both look up from the phone as Bree gestures back at the stove that I honestly had no idea worked. Guess it does the way the water is boiling over the pot. "We're making spaghetti."

"What's with the phone?" I place my purse on the counter.

Rhys grunts, "Directions."

I don't think spaghetti is all that complicated to make, but what the hell do I know. "The sauce smells good."

Bree moves over to the stove, stirring the sauce. "It's from a jar."

Rhys puts his phone down, grabbing a package of pasta. "I guess we just boil it."

Bree nods, and I try not to smile too big. Pretty sure it would piss them both off, but even so, I think it's cute, them making dinner together.

After we eat the dinner they prepared—that was surprisingly tasty—Bree heads up to her room to work on homework. Leaving me and Rhys in the kitchen to clean up. It's strange how comfortable acting like a family is.

The doorbell rings, and I nearly drop a plate in the sink at the sound. "Who the hell could that be?"

Rhys looks stiff as he dries his hands. "I don't know, but I have a pretty good idea."

The social worker.

We make our way to the door and sure enough, when Rhys opens the door, a stern looking woman with an iPad is standing at the door. "May I come in?"

Rhys grunts in response, and I'm the one who supplies the actual answer. "Yes. Please come in." If my spoiled upbringing taught me anything, it's being a good hostess. I can fake it with the best of them.

She slips inside, and I close the door behind her, putting my best cheesy smile on. "Bree is upstairs doing homework, and Rhys and I were in the kitchen, cleaning up after dinner."

She studies me, pulling something up on her iPad. "I'll need to talk to her in a moment." Her eyes survey the living room. "I need to see the entire home to ensure her safety."

"Of course." I place my hand over my chest, still giving a performance suitable for an Emmy. "I absolutely love giving tours. I swipe my hand in front of me like a game show presenter. "This is the living room, as you can tell." I gesture for her to follow, and she does, along with Rhys who looks sick.

I show her the basement with a family room and gym before taking her back up to the kitchen. I nod toward the stairs. "All the bedrooms are up here."

"I'll follow you." She hasn't warmed up in the slightest, and I don't like the way she's looking at Rhys. Like a bug. One she wants to smoosh under her shoe.

I lead her up to Bree's room and am sure to knock first, waiting for Bree's reply before we walk in. "Bree, I think you already know Ms. Winters." The social worker bitch that shook Rhys's confidence.

Of course, I can't say that last part.

Bree just nods from her place on the bed. "Good evening, Bree." Now this woman sounds like Cinderella when she talks to Bree, leaning down and looking into her eyes. Jesus.

Bree is not having it. "Hey."

"How was school?"

I look over at Rhys, who looks like he's about to break his teeth if he clenches his jaw any tighter.

Bree shrugs, what she always does. "Fine."

The social worker looks around the room. When I took her shopping, I finally talked Bree into a comforter that said more "preteen" and less "adult guest." It's hot pink with black squiggles. I bought the matching curtains, but we haven't had a chance to put them up yet.

"How do you like your room?"

Again with the shoulder lift. She really could pass for Rhys's biological daughter. "It's fine."

"Aubrey, you can be honest with me."

I feel Rhys tense, and I automatically hate this bitch. "Of course, you can. We were about to finish the tour. You wanna come, Bree?"

Her eyes dart to mine, and she shakes her head, but her chin is lifted, showing her strength. "No. That sounds boring. I have homework."

Good girl. Use words.

I laugh at that and shake my head. "Alright then." I smile big toward the social worker, gesturing for her to follow. I show her my office, and then we go to the master bedroom.

"This is our room." The room is pristine. The bed made, and Rhys's stuff put away in the dresser I had ordered. I guess it was here when he got in today. The duffle bag he was living out of is out of sight.

He must have sensed the visit was coming because the blanket he uses to sleep with on the chaise lounge has been put up. Ms. Winters looks around. "Is there anything inappropriate for an eleven-year-old in here?"

"You mean like porn?" My filter failed me as she turns to look at me.

"As long as it's safely away, that shouldn't be a problem. Along with any other . . ." she eyes Rhys hard, "sordid items."

She thinks Rhys is kinky. Ha. I want to laugh, considering he won't let me touch him. "Nothing sordid in here," I say, fingering the rose pendant around my neck.

"Guns?"

"No," Rhys answers, his tone has a definite edge to it.

"Drugs?" Now she's trying her best to show Rhys how much she despises him, and it makes me seethe with fury.

"No. Rhys is clean. Why would we have drugs or even alcohol in the house?"

She knows he's an addict. I can feel it. The way she said the word "drugs" as if she's waiting for him to mess up. She fiddles with the iPad in her hands. "Okay. I'm going to go have a conversation with Bree." She pins Rhys with a hard look. "Alone."

We both nod as she leaves the bedroom, and I face Rhys. "Jesus Christ, what is up her ass?"

"She thinks I took a good thing away from Bree."

"Getting molested by a sick motherfucker isn't robbing her of anything good, Rhys. Nothing is worth that."

I watch his throat bob, and I want to comfort the asshole, but I know I can't with a touch. "Fuck her. We're going to win this."

"It's not a game, Blair."

"Everything is a game, Rhys. You have to play to win, or you'll lose every time."

We walk down the hall after waiting a few minutes, and Ms. Winters leaves the room, waving to Bree with fake, ridiculous vigor.

"I'll be back to check in very soon, Mr. Moore."

"We'll be here," Rhys seethes, and I play my part as we walk her to the door, putting a smile on my face.

"This is a nice home you have here. How long have you two been together again?"

She looks at the gap between my body, and Rhys and I know

she's implying we aren't a real couple, like she's catching us in a lie. I quickly wrap my arm around Rhys, who recoils, but I hold him to me, laying my head on his shoulder.

I swear I can hear his heart beating from here, but I'm hoping he'll play along.

"Three years," I say with a purr, looking up at him. Rhys looks pale, and his body is so fucking tense as I lean against him.

She studies us intently, her gaze falling where I touch him, and I can hear him breathing deep to keep from freaking out. My heart aches for him.

"You applied for long term foster care. Do you have any plans to marry?"

Now my body feels just as tense as Rhys's, but I recover even when he doesn't. "I mean, who needs that? The whole thing seems pretty outdated to me." I drag my free hand over Rhys's arms, and I'm hoping she doesn't hear the sharp intake of his breath from the contact. "We're committed, that's all that matters."

Her lips purse as she types something on her tablet. "I see."

Shit. Did I say something wrong? They can't deny him because of that, can they?

"I'll be back soon."

"You said that already," Rhys spits, and I tighten my hold to rein him in.

She leaves, and I quickly release him to close the door before turning back to him. "You have to be nice, Rhys. Kiss some ass."

"I don't do that," he says through clenched teeth, and I wonder if he's still wound tight from my touch.

"You think I like that? Newsflash, I hate being nice."

"Yeah. No shit. So why were you?"

"It's part of the game." I walk toward him, and he steps back quickly, his hands in front of him like he's afraid I'm going to touch him again. I try not to let that sting.

"Relax. I only did that for show. She doesn't think we're a real couple."

"We aren't."

I glare at him, annoyed that he can't just try to be fucking human for a moment. "I know that, but she's supposed to think we are. Get it together."

He takes a seat on the bottom of the stairs, and again, I feel that stabbing feeling in my heart as he fists his hair, leaving his elbows propped up on his knees.

I take a seat on the step below him so I don't touch him. "Rhys, do I get another question?"

He looks down at me where I sit, his gaze looking like he thinks I'm crazy. "After all that?"

"I mean, I did well. I think I should get a reward."

He groans and lets go of his hair. "What?"

"You said the last foster home was the worst one." He looks pale again, maybe even green, so I quickly ask my question. "What was the best one?"

"That's like asking about my favorite trip to the hospital."

This time I'm the one to wince, and I hate it. I don't like that he's had more than one trip to the hospital or that he had such a horrible childhood, but still there had to be something good. "So, what's the answer?"

He takes in a big breath, his massive chest filling out even more before he lets it go. "I don't know. There was one I was in when I was eight. I was there with Sean at the same time. The foster dad was a trucker, so he wasn't home a lot, and the mom was batty as all fuck. But Sean was there, so it wasn't so bad."

I smile. "See, that wasn't so hard."

His eyes roll as he stands. "Thanks for taking it easy on me."

I want to know so much. I need to know why I can't touch him, but I don't push it. Not tonight.

But I will find out.

Rhys

"I have good news for you." I'm waiting for Bree to get out of school as I hold the phone to my ear.

"Okay."

Gillian goes on. "So you're approved for long-term care and can keep Bree for now."

I don't like the for now part. "But?"

"We don't need to get ahead of ourselves, Rhys. This is a win. You and Bree did well with the first two inspections."

The social worker bitch showed up again three days after the first visit to talk to Bree and I guess to try to catch us in some drug-infused orgy party. When really, we were all just sitting in the living room quietly watching some annoying show on MTV Blair and Bree like. "Just tell me, Gillian."

She sighs into the phone. "Mr. Herrington could fight it. He was starting the adoption process the day Bree showed up at your shop. He could still try."

"So, what now?" My entire body tenses up, and I see Bree walking with the two guys she's usually with.

"Social services has to finish their investigation of him before he can push forward with that, but I don't think he's going to just give up."

I know he won't.

"An investigation like that can take a while." But not if you can grease the right palms.

"Only time will tell, Rhys. All you can do right now is be the best foster parent possible. Stay out of trouble."

I grunt into the phone, and her voice is kind, almost soothing.

"I know this is difficult. We'll talk soon. Okay?"

I nod my head even if she can't see me. "Okay."

We get off the phone just as Bree opens the back door and climbs in, her little friends waving to her and eying me suspiciously.

"What are their names?"

I navigate my way out of the school parking lot, and she answers with an annoyed tone. "Fletcher and Rhett."

"Who are they to you?" I try to keep my voice casual, but I see her eyes roll in my rearview mirror.

"Friends. We met in the group home, but we go to school together."

Group home. Fuck. So, they're foster kids too. Makes sense. We tend to keep to our own. Instinct for safety.

She puts her headphones in until we reach my shop. Last week, I closed up early, and we just went back to Blair's after school. But I can't afford to keep doing that, so she's been hanging out at the shop this week until Blair picks her up after work.

We go inside, and she makes herself comfortable on the couch meant for customers, taking out a book and her headphones, but she looks up at me as I prepare to reopen.

"Rhys?"

I look over at her. "What's up?"

"Why are you doing this?"

I try to offer the simple answer, hoping she'll accept it because, let's face it, this is Bree. She likes to talk about as much as I do. "You asked me for help."

She lifts a questioning eyebrow "You always help everyone who asks for it?"

"No." That's the simple answer, and I add, "You're special."

"I'm a handful," she grumbles as she searches for something—

probably a song—on her phone. "That's what they all say. All my files describe me as a handful. School. Social workers."

"They're all idiots. You haven't been a handful for us."

My saying "us" kind of surprises me, but I know Blair likes Bree too. She's embraced having her around.

I walk to where she's sitting, and I crouch down in front of her, not touching her of course, but I want her to see my eyes, and I want to see hers. "Do you want to stay with me longer?" She looks cautious. "I was approved for long-term foster care today. And you can, if you want to."

She just lifts her shoulders, feigning indifference that was learned long ago even if she's only eleven. "That would be okay."

I nod my head in decision. "Good. I want you to."

A small smile graces her face as she puts her headphones back in and holds her book in front of her face.

I have no idea what I'm doing, but today, I feel good.

Blair

"So, he can just adopt her? Even though she's in our custody?"

"Technically, she's still a ward of the state. So, I don't know."

I stare at him, annoyed that he doesn't seem more worked up. I mean, this was his fucking idea in the first place. He brought this little girl here. And god damn if I didn't go ahead and fall for the little brat. I mean, how could you not?

She's tough. I have no idea the horrors she's seen in her short life, but she has a sweet side. And a funny side. I like hanging out with her when I pick her up from Rhys's shop after work. She humors me and goes shopping with me. We watch trashy TV together. She won't talk about boys with me yet, but I'm oddly excited about that part.

And now, Rhys is telling me that the motherfucker she's afraid of can just take her away? No way.

"So what? We just sit here and wait around?"

He turns to me, and I see the defeat in his eyes. Bree is asleep—at least her little butt better be asleep. She has school tomorrow. And we're in my room. His body is stretched out on the ridiculous chair as I lie on the bed facing him, already under the covers.

"Yes." His voice is strained.

"That's fucking stupid."

I can tell his patience with me is growing thin. He tucks his inked, heavily muscled arm under his head as he looks over at me. "I know that. All I can do is follow their rules and wait for the investigation to be completed. You're the one who told me to play the fucking game."

"I know, but sitting around isn't playing." I sit up, bracing my weight on one arm and don't miss his eyes roaming over my body. I really hate wearing clothes to bed, but for him I do it. Still, pretty much everything I have is sexy, and tonight I'm wearing a black lacy cami and shorts. Even though I'm worried about Bree, I can't deny his gaze makes me hot. "Gillian can't do anything?"

"It's not her case. Or even her city. I can't have her getting in trouble for me. She's already sticking her neck out." He looks twitchy and uncomfortable as he sits up. The blanket drops to his waist, and I shamelessly let my eyes drift over his ripped muscles cultivated from hours in the gym.

I don't even care that I'm flat-out gawking. I'm stressed, and although I usually use sex to help calm me down, the hard edge in the look on his face tells me he's not in the mood.

"I need to look into a private school for her."

That catches me off guard. "What? Why would you do that?" She likes her school from what I've gathered.

He shrugs, his large shoulders lifting in indifference, but I can tell he feels anything but that. "She deserves to have good shit. Fancy."

I know I can't touch him, but I see the struggle in him. That fucking social worker really got to him. I fling the covers completely off my body and walk across the room to sit on the end of his chair. "No. She doesn't. Have you met the girl?"

He's too serious as he looks at me. "I have. She's a good kid who had a shitty start. I don't want to rob her of having good things, Blair."

"She doesn't need a fancy school or clothes to have it good. I grew up that way."

His brow furrows, and I think it's cute that he's trying to focus on this subject and not on my chest. "And now you live here." He gestures around the massive bedroom. "And you drive a Mercedes. I grew up in a public school system and struggle to keep my head above water."

It pains me that he seems to value his worth at so little. "You own your own business."

His eyes meet mine with a sadness that sends a dagger through my heart, and then he shakes it off. "I don't like the way the boys look at her at that school."

I can't help it. I laugh at him. I cover my mouth and try to stop it, but I can't. "Aw, you're in full-on dad mode now."

"Shut up." He tosses a pillow at me, and I laugh, catching it and holding it to my body.

"Private school boys will be looking at her too. They're all the same. Rich boys may be even worse." The ones I've met like to collect women as possessions, and I shudder to think of Bree meeting any men like that.

"I don't want her to feel robbed."

God, I want to touch him. I want to lay on that broad chest and listen to his heartbeat like some pathetic woman fascinated by a man. Which repulses me, but also excites me.

I wish he would let me touch him.

"Rhys?" He's lost in thought, looking out the window, but he looks back at me.

"What?"

I bite my bottom lip, watching him with need. I've never had to really make the first move before. It's just always been offered, but with Rhys, the fucker makes me work for it.

So, I usually just go the overly horny route, shielding my heart by using over-the-top antics that should humiliate me. I let his pillow drop to the floor and let my palms rest on both sides of his ankles, bunching my tits together. "I'm stressed the fuck out."

"You look fine." It's flippant and annoying, trying to shoo me away.

I just lean into it. "I'm horny."

He leans his head back against the chair. "You're always horny."

"As are most fucking dudes." I fling one hand in irritation that he doesn't want me nearly as bad as I want him. I try to soften my approach, knowing he clearly has intimacy issues. "You know your dick works with me."

We've proven that many times. As long as I don't look into his eyes or touch him, we're good.

"Blair, I'm tired."

And it's not from lack of sleep. That's not the type of tired he is, and it's evident from his voice.

I wish he would just let me touch him. Let me make him feel better. Fuck, I would even settle for just spooning with his grumpy ass.

And I've never wanted to do that before.

"Too tired to fuck?" I want to crawl up his body, but I don't. I do, however, lift my top off and toss it to the floor behind me, leaving my chest bare for him. "I'll do all the work."

"Why?"

Seriously? I'm half naked and begging to fuck him, and he's asking me why? Jesus Christ, why can't I like an easy guy? There are a ton of them. But nooooo . . . Blair wants the complicated, big, moody motherfucker.

"Why what?"

"Why are you so fucking willing to please me? To do everything I want you to. My way."

"Have you met me? I don't cater to anyone."

He leans his body forward, but he's still too far away. "You do for me."

"And that's why you deny me? Because I'm too fucking easy?"

He looks at my chest, unable to stop himself now that my breasts are out on display, but then drags his gaze back up to my face. "Is that tonight's question?"

I fold my arms over my ample chest, feeling vulnerable and agitated by the pending answer already, not even knowing what it is. "Yes."

He huffs and scoots so his body is only a few inches from

mine. I can feel his heat, and I crave his touch as much as I want to touch him. "I think you're better than this. I think you have a tough exterior, but inside is a little girl who just wants to please and who thinks using her body is the only way to get male attention."

My eyes widen as I look him in the eyes no matter how much his words sting. "Fuck you. There's nothing wrong with a woman liking sex."

"No there's not. But think back, Blair. To every guy you've ever fucked." I swallow and brace myself. "Did you really want them? Every one of them? Or were you trying to replace something you weren't getting? Trying to get daddy's attention? Trying to get men's attention? Logan's?"

"You think that's what I'm doing with you?"

He doesn't move. Only holds my gaze. "I don't know. But can you tell me that all of that was for you?"

No. I'm the spoiled little rich girl acting out, trying desperately to get her father's attention when he couldn't give a fuck about me. He never could. And no matter how much I've acted out, he still doesn't care. "Orgasms are orgasms."

"So, they all made you come?"

Not even close.

He closes his eyes and takes a deep breath before lifting his lids slowly and using his hand to sweep across my cheek. His touch is gentle, and my heart squeezes tightly in my chest from the contact I crave. "You deserve better than letting me use you like a sex doll. You deserve someone who can touch you and hold you."

He's never been this open and honest with me. This sweet. I don't really know how to handle it as he drops his hand to his lap.

"You can touch me all you want."

He swallows, and I know he can't. He definitely can't let me reciprocate, and I have no idea why.

He dips down and hands my top to me, his eyes scanning over my face and my chest, but he looks tortured. "I think I need to buy you some real fucking pajamas."

I shove the lacey camisole over my head and glare at him. "These are pajamas. For grownups. That. Fuck. And like to fuck."

He's not thrown off by my bratty behavior. He knew I would throw a fit.

"If I didn't want you to touch me, I wouldn't ask for it, Rhys. I'm a grown woman. Don't tell me what I want and don't want. You didn't have any problem fucking me in the country club bathroom not that long ago."

He leans close again, the scent of him wafting toward me. "You want that forever, Blair? You want to face away from me, palms against the wall while I slam into you, trying my best not to touch you too much because I'm too afraid of freaking out or losing my erection when memories slam into me harder than I'm slamming into you? You want that for what? A month? A year? How long until you get sick of being used that way?"

He's furious and scared. I see the deep, deep scars under the surface, and he only gets more pissed as he climbs off the chair. I don't know what to say.

But it doesn't matter because he leaves my room before I can come up with anything.

And I'm vile because all I want is for him to come back regardless of what we do, I just want him near.

Rhys

I'M LOSING my fucking mind. Not that I ever really had control of it. Blair is still pissy after the other night, and I don't fucking blame her.

Why I can't just throw her down on the bed and fuck her is beyond me. I mean, I know why.

Fuck, I'm losing it.

Not to mention every day that goes by, I'm just more and more worried about Herrington trying to adopt Bree.

Bree and Blair are sitting on the couch, hanging out when I come home from work. It all seems so fucking normal.

Which is bizarre. Blair is glaring daggers at me, and I get it. I nod a hello to Bree who gives me a quick wave as I hear my phone in my pocket.

I pull it out and see Sean's name and almost smile. I haven't talked to him in weeks. I hit answer as I start up the stairs. "You're allowed to call?"

He just laughs in that easy Sean way I hate to admit I fucking miss. "Fuck you, asshole. These phones work both ways."

"Yeah. Yeah." I walk into Blair's bedroom and take a seat on my chair. "What's up?"

"Really? You aren't going to tell me?"

Well, fuck. "What?"

"Don't play dumb with me. You're a foster parent now? And with Blair, the she-demon herself, no less."

I lean back with a groan. "How the fuck do you know that?"

I can hear his eye roll over the phone. "You called Gillian. She, of course called Logan, who told Quinn, who told my fucking wife. But the real question is why the fuck you didn't call me first so I could tell you that was a terrible fucking idea."

That's exactly why I didn't call him. "Well, now you know."

"No. Don't do that short-sentence Rhys bullshit with me." Motherfucker, sometimes I hate my best friend. "What the hell are you thinking?"

"I'm thinking the kid needed my help. She begged me to help her. What the fuck was I supposed to do, Sean?"

He's quiet for a minute. "Needed your help why?"

"I don't know. I haven't really asked her, but she was afraid of her foster dad, and you and I both know what that's like."

"This can't be good for you, Rhys."

He knows most of my dark secrets, and I know he felt responsible for keeping me sober all those years. And when I wasn't sober, he cleaned me up. Every fucking time. No matter if I was getting into fights or laying in my own puke. He was there. "I'm fine."

"Bullshit." He doesn't miss a beat. "Taking in an abused foster kid? This has to be bringing up memories for you."

My hand clenches around the phone, and my stomach roils. "I'm going to meetings."

"You been talking?"

Fucker. "I've been going."

"Rhys . . ." He's careful with his words. "I'm all for you helping out a kid like us. But goddammit, if you let this wreck you, I swear I'll fly down there and kick your ass."

"You can try, you scrawny motherfucker."

He laughs. "Scrawny hell. I'll whip your big ass."

"She needs my help." I sound weak, and I know he can hear it. My appetite has been next to nothing since I took her in, the nightmares have increased, and I've spent a lot of time at the gym. But I need her in my life. I need to help her.

Nothing is going to change that.

"Just keep going to your fucking meetings."

I just went last week, but I may need to increase my frequency even if I don't really believe in them. "I will."

"If you feel yourself drowning, call someone in to pull you out. You hear me?"

"I do."

He doesn't believe me, but he knows me well enough to know I'm not backing down. "Okay. I'll be in touch."

We hang up, and I hear Blair at the door seconds before she walks in and sits down next to me on the chair. "Sean?"

"Eavesdropping?"

She lifts her shoulder. "No, I was just texting with Mel. She's upset that I didn't tell her about Bree."

That is surprising. I'm pretty sure they tell each other everything.

"Why didn't you?"

"I didn't want her to talk me out of it." One thing about Blair, she's always honest.

"Yeah. I get that."

"Question time?" Her eyebrow lifts as she watches me with curiosity, and I'm worried about the question.

"I guess."

"If Gillian told them about Bree, does that mean she's worried about the investigation?"

I should be relieved she's not asking about my past, but the question only causes pain in my gut.

"Yeah. I think so."

She looks as defeated as I feel, which I don't like seeing. I want her tough and angry, ready to fight.

"We can't lose her, Rhys." Her eyes lock on mine. "I'll do anything to keep her."

"I know." I want to tease her about falling for the kid, but this isn't funny. I don't want to lose Bree either. I really don't want to hand her over to that motherfucker.

I'll die before I allow that to happen.

Blair

WE'RE BOTH COMPLETELY STRESSED, and it appears Gillian is feeling the same way. She drove in today for a meeting with us and Ms. Winters, who I still want to tit punch.

Her steely eyes haven't left Rhys since we sat down, and we both know that them calling this meeting isn't a good thing.

"What's going on?" Rhys asks the question that's on the tip of my tongue.

Ms. Winters, the cold bitch, is the one all too happy to answer. "The investigation into Mr. Herrington has been completed."

What's it been? A month? Seems they don't have any problem moving their asses when money is involved. I watch the news. I know how backed up social services is. One month to conclude what? "And?" I ask, my voice far too nervous sounding.

"And nothing. The investigation revealed nothing other than two loving parents who wanted to add to their family."

"And what Bree said holds no weight?" I see the tension in Rhys's jaw, and I know he's close to snapping.

"Of course, it does." Gillian's sweet voice is a contrast to Morgan's. "All this means is he's been cleared of any wrongdoing."

"And he can file for adoption now?" I ask, my stomach in knots. I don't want to lose her.

"Yes." She nods her head slowly, sweeping her blond hair behind her ear, and I can tell she's anxious about this as well.

"Why wouldn't he?" Ms. Winter's has my attention as my head swivels to look at her with the disdain I feel. "They would be good for that child. And there really isn't anything you can do about this."

Rhys's eyes meet Gillian's, and she looks sympathetic. "That's not necessarily true."

Morgan gives her a dirty look, but I feel hopeful as I look to Gillian. "What can we do?"

"Nothing. You can and should do nothing." Ms. Winters is getting all worked up now, but I couldn't give a shit.

"I was asking Gillian," I say, a bitchy edge to my voice, and again, I don't care.

Gillian clears her throat and looks between me and Rhys. "You have the advantage. You can file for adoption too."

Ms. Winters looks absolutely horrified, and it makes me smile as Rhys shifts in his chair, looking far more beaten down than I would like. "Adopt her?"

Gillian nods, her head tilted slightly to the side. I know she has a soft spot for Rhys even if they barely know each other. She's Logan's stepmother after all. "Yes. Adopt her."

"That's absurd and completely unorthodox."

Gillian looks at her colleague who, according to Rhys, she thought she could trust. "I realize that this is your case, but if you aren't going to supply them with all of the necessary information, I'm happy to take over. I'm sure Marion would be fine with that."

I have no idea who Marion is, but if I had to guess, it's their boss. She huffs and stands up. "Fine. I have other work to do but know I will be in any hearing involving Aubrey."

Rhys snarls at her, but to his credit, he's quiet as she exits.

And finally, it's just Gillian and us. Gillian has a far more calming presence. "Okay you guys, I'm not going to lie to you. This won't be a cakewalk. The Herringtons have a lot of money and pull in the community."

I see Rhys's face turn pale, and I resist rubbing his back or touching his thigh as I face Gillian head-on. "We can file to adopt her though?"

"Yes. You can. She's in your care right now, which leaves you at a certain advantage, along with the fact that she likes you guys, I'm assuming."

I smile and Rhys just grunts. "As much as she can."

I roll my eyes. "She loves us."

Gillian smiles. "Okay. Good. That's very good. She's eleven, almost twelve, so the judge should take her opinion into consideration."

Rhys's spine is eerily straight. "But they might not."

Gillian sighs. "They might not. Look, a hearing, no matter how much money is involved, is at least three months away. I can't imagine they could rush it any more than that. That gives you guys time."

"For?" I know Rhys feels defeated but my question arises from the hopeful feeling inside me.

"To look as good on paper as you possibly can."

Rhys snorts. "Well, I'm fucked."

I give him a look, annoyed with his defeated attitude, and Gillian just shakes her head. "No. You're not. You own your own business."

"Brand new, and it was handed to me." Rhys places his hands on the table between us and Gillian and looks up at the ceiling.

"It's in your name, Rhys. And Chris will back you up."

His eyes snap to hers. "I don't need him to back me up." She goes to cover his hand, and he jerks it away quickly. She looks slightly stunned, and I want to tell her he just has a weird thing with touching, but I don't want to piss him off.

She recovers quickly though. "It doesn't matter. On paper, you're a business owner, and it's doing well. You have no criminal record."

He snorts again. "I should."

"But you don't. Your record is clean." She holds up her hands in rebuttal. "And don't tell me about any illegal things you've been involved in. As long as there isn't a record, then you're fine."

He swallows, and I watch the movement while Gillian continues.

"You have Bree, who wants to be with you. And Blair is employed and quite frankly, an Ashton."

Normally I hate my last name and the pull it has, no matter how much I appear to love my spoiled little rich girl persona, but right now I feel a sense of relief. "My last name can help?'

She nods. "When you're going against a Herrington? Yes."

"That's fucked up," Rhys says, making my cheeks flame with embarrassment. I know how he feels about the rich and privileged.

"If it can help, it can help. I'm not losing her." I turn my head back to focus only on Gillian. "What else?"

She looks nervous now. "Well, the only thing they have over you two, is they're married."

I almost gulp, and I can feel Rhys stiffen next to me. "No fucking way."

She gathers the folders that are in front of her. "I know. It's a big step, but it will go a long way in your favor if you're married and adopting her together."

I don't dare look at Rhys. "A long way?"

Gillian looks at us both affectionately. "Yes. A very long way. I don't see how they could deny you as long as no one gets into trouble before then and you're married."

Rhys is silent as Gillian rises. "I've done as much as I can. Morgan's right, she'll be the one called to speak at the hearing. All I can do is advise you to think very hard about how badly you want to keep Bree from the Herringtons. This is a huge decision, and I know neither of you will take it lightly."

"Thank you, Gillian." I stand, and she gives me a hug.

She doesn't touch Rhys, who is still sitting down, but she waves sympathetically to him before she exits.

"Don't even think about it, Blair."

I'm annoyed with him as I sit back down, facing him as I sit sideways in my chair. "We have to. You heard her."

He turns to look at me, his eyes hard. "You want to fucking marry me? Me?"

"Yes." I answer with no hesitation, and he looks horrified. "I want Bree safe."

"This isn't playing house, Blair. Or even a fucking game. This is her life. This is permanent. This is us getting married and having a kid."

I hate how disgusted he sounds at the thought, but I push through for her. "I love her. And don't fucking make fun of me . . ." He just stares. "This is your fault. I shouldn't have gotten all attached, but I did. I want her."

"And me?" His voice is hoarse.

I don't know how to answer that. I don't know if there's actually a future with Rhys considering he won't let me in and he won't let me touch him, but I do care about him. "It's paperwork."

"Blair . . ." His elbows drop to the table in front of him. "I can't do this."

"Yes. You can."

"I can't rob you of your life too."

God, he thinks being married to him would be a prison. "Look, Rhys." I almost reach for him, but I stop myself. He must have sensed it because he drops his arms flat on the table and turns to look at me. "You're a broody asshole. And a real pain. But you're not bad to look at, you seem to have a good heart in there as evidenced by you wanting to save Bree, and . . ." I shrug, "you're a good fuck when you want to be."

He rolls his eyes, and I laugh, but he doesn't look mad. "Marriage is a big deal."

"Only if we make it that way. I wasn't planning on ever getting married, but who cares? If we can save her, let's do it."

He swivels his body to completely face me. "You really want to do this?"

"Yes." I say it instantly with a smile, never wavering. "I do."

"You'll regret this."

I know I won't. As long as we get Bree and ensure her safety, I don't care what happens to my heart.

Rhys

SHE HAS OFFICIALLY LOST her fucking mind. I mean, I want to protect Bree more than anyone, but marriage? This has gotten out of control.

By the time we leave the social services office, it's time to pick up Bree. After dropping off Blair's car at the house, we swing by the school, but we're a few minutes early.

"Talk to me."

I look over at her, surprised she's still trying. I don't get it. "About what? Getting legally fucking married to each other?"

"Yes." She looks down at her phone. "It says here Missouri has no wait time on a marriage license. We can go tomorrow, get our license, and be married by a judge before noon."

Jesus fucking Christ. She holds up her phone, showing me the official website she has open. I just lean my head back and try to take some deep breaths.

Married. As in actually married.

That's something I never planned to be. I look up in time to see Bree walking out toward the pickup line with both boys in tow. They're always by her side, and it shouldn't, but it fucking irks me.

"God, they're cute." I turn to look at Blair, annoyed by her statement.

"They're twelve."

She laughs. "I mean the three of them, best friends for life. And yeah, you can already tell they're all going to be devastatingly beautiful."

My hands clench tightly around the steering wheel as Bree and the boys, Fletcher and Rhett, stand beside the car, joking around. Even I have to admit, it's good to see Bree being a kid with a smile on her face. These boys seem to be able to do that for her.

I roll down the window. "Come on. We can't hold up the line."

Blair shoots me an annoyed look. "Damn. Chill, Dad."

"That's what I'll be if we go through with this." I keep my voice low, and Blair just shrugs me off. Bree rolls her eyes at me from outside the car, waves goodbye to the boys, and climbs in the back seat.

"Why are you both here?"

My body tenses, but Blair turns around in her seat to look back at Bree. "We had a meeting with the social worker bitch."

Bree visibly straightens in her seat, and I know she's worried but is trying to remain calm on the outside. "What did she want?"

I hear the quivering in her voice even though she's trying her best to hide it. I exit the school parking lot and glance at Blair, signaling for her to tell her.

Blair is still twisted in her seat looking back at her. "Mr. Herrington and his wife are moving forward with applying for adoption."

I hear the sharp intake of air and the unmistakable fear in her eyes as I look through the rearview mirror. "What?"

"We aren't going to let it happen," I say definitively, "ever."

"That's right." I can see Blair's smile directed toward Bree from the corner of my eye as I drive back to Blair's house. Her voice, however, is cautious. "How would you feel about us adopting you instead?"

I don't want to look at her face, but my own curiosity gets me as I watch her in the mirror. "You guys want to adopt me? Like not just foster me?"

Blair gives a firm nod, portraying the confidence Bree needs which I don't have. "Yes. It would be official. We'd be your parents according to the law."

"So, I wouldn't be in the system anymore?"

"No. Never again." I meet her eyes in the mirror and am surprised when I see a small smile form on her lips.

But it fades as she looks out the window, her voice quiet, "Why would you guys want to adopt an eleven-year-old?"

Blair looks at me, confusion on her gorgeous face, but I know why Bree's asking. Growing up, it was pretty much a given that if you weren't adopted before you were old enough to talk, you were fucked. Adoptive parents all wanted babies. "Why wouldn't we want not only an eleven-year-old," Blair looks back at Bree, "but the world's coolest eleven-year-old?"

Bree smiles and shakes her head. "You're so lame."

Blair doesn't take that as an insult and get pissy, she laughs so easily instead. And I know she really has fallen for the kid. Nothing is going to stop her.

"We want you Bree," I add as I pull into Blair's driveway.

I turn around to face Bree as she fidgets with the hem of her t-shirt. "So, if you adopt me, he can't?"

The way she says "he" makes me sick to my stomach. "He" would be her monster. She doesn't want to say his name. She doesn't want him to be real.

Blair winces only slightly, but Bree picks up on it instantly, using her ability to read people. "What?"

I clear my throat and fight the itching, sickening feeling inside me, the urge to use and numb myself from memories that threaten to creep up when I see how afraid she is of her monster. "There will be a hearing since two couples want to adopt you, but we'll win."

"How can you be so sure?"

Blair answers with fierce reassurance, "Because we will do everything we can to make sure we do, Bree. Everything. You'll never have to leave us."

Bree looks frightened, but she seems to trust in Blair's words too. At least she wants to, I can see that. "Okay." Her voice is too meek for her.

"We're going to make sure we win." I lock eyes with her, begging her to believe me. "I want this so fucking bad that I've agree to marry her." I point to Blair, and Bree's eyes widen.

"Gee thanks, asshole," Blair says, but she's smiling. "And I'm going to marry this broody fucker just for you."

"You guys are getting married?" She actually laughs at that, and the sound is beautiful, hitting me right in the chest.

"Yeah." I look at Blair. "Tomorrow?"

She nods her head as her eyes meet mine. "Tomorrow. The sooner the better." She looks back at Bree. "We have to make sure we are the best possible choice on paper."

"Okay, cool." Bree opens her door, swinging her backpack over her shoulder and climbs out, closing the door behind her.

"It's going to be okay, Rhys." Blair is watching Bree walk up to the house. She has a key and uses it to go inside.

"You sure about this? You'll be married to me, Blair."

She lets her head rest against the back of the seat. "I know that." She turns to look at me, not lifting her head. "I'll do anything to protect her, even marry someone else and adopt her with him if you won't."

A smile tugs at my lips, liking this side of Blair, a side that was always there, I just didn't let myself analyze it.

"You're kind of ruining your rep, you know?"

"As the bitch who doesn't give a fuck?"

I nod, but I try to add a small smile. Her hand starts toward my face, but I fucking flinch away from her, and I hate myself for doing it. She drops her hand and plays it off, grabbing her car door and pushing it open.

"It's just paperwork, Rhys. It's not a big deal, we're already living together."

I tell myself that's true as she climbs out and goes inside. I lay my head against the steering wheel and take deep breaths.

In. And. Out.
You can do this.

Rhys

I STARE in the mirror in Blair's massive master bathroom. I'm still shirtless after my shower, and I look at the hard muscles of my chest and stomach. My arms are flexed tight, showing the sinewy lines carved from hours at the gym, but it all sickens me.

I never feel bulked-up enough. I never feel strong enough.

I grip the marble countertop in front of the sink, trying to tell myself to breathe. That it's just on paper, but it's marriage. It's official. And it's adoption. I'm going to be Bree's father if this all works out.

My stomach revolts, and I barely make it to the toilet before spilling the minimal food I managed to choke down at breakfast. "Fuck!"

I sit on the cool tile of the floor and lean back against the wall, waiting for another round when Blair walks in, looking so very fucking Blair. She's wearing a flesh colored minidress, if it can be called that, that clings to every single curve she has. And she'll be lucky if she doesn't break her neck walking up the stairs of the courthouse in those beige high heels. Her full tits are on full display, her hair is down with soft blond waves, and she looks fucking phenomenal. But I feel like shit as I look up at her.

"Jesus Blair, I think I can see your clit from here."

She rolls her eyes and tugs subconsciously on the skirt that's not really that short. I'm just being a dick. "Please don't make me kick you in the balls when you're already down."

I flush the toilet and climb up from the floor, pushing past her. "Is that your version of white?" I grab my toothbrush and paste.

She looks down at the dress and shrugs. "It's nude. More fitting for me, I think. And don't pretend you don't think I look hot as fuck." She does. She always does. Her head nods at my bare chest as I brush my teeth. "You going for the naked look too?"

I shrug my shoulders and spit the toothpaste into the sink. "Maybe."

"Rhys, just talk to me. I'm about to be your wife."

I splash cold water on my face, dry it with a towel and then turn around to face her as I lean back against the counter. "You can still get out of it."

"No fucking way." She folds her arms over her ample chest. I already knew that was coming. "I never thought I'd get married."

"Yeah, me fucking either." She stands inches in front of me, standing tall and confident, dressed up and ready. "But we're doing this for Bree."

I nod my head as she goes to the door handle, where the navy button-down shirt she bought for today is hanging. She takes it off the hanger and hands it to me.

"As much as I hate to see you cover up . . ." I take it and shake my head at her as I slide into the sleeves and button the shirt.

"Always so fucking horny."

She laughs. "Well, I have a fiancé who won't fuck me."

She's joking, but it sends a jolt through me. She's about to marry a guy who can barely stand to touch her long enough to come during sex. How long can she be happy with that? Who the fuck could be satisfied with a life like that?

"Blair." Her eyes snap to mine as I finish dressing. "You don't have to do this. We can find another way."

"Stop trying to talk me out of this. I want this."

I swallow, trying to keep it together. "I'm fucked-up. I'll never be able to give you what you need."

We can say this is only "on paper" all we want, but I know there are some real feelings there. I know she cares about me, and I fucking hate it. I wish I could make them disappear for her sake. "You're giving me Bree."

"But we both know that won't be enough."

Her hand ghosts over my face without making any actual contact, and with watery eyes, she lets air escape her lungs softly. "We can do this. And we'll figure it out. All of it. Right now, we just have to do what we can to get her safe."

"You're already a good mom."

She smiles as she drops her hand to her side, but she looks nervous as she meets my eyes again. "Rhys . . . before we get married, I need to know."

I nearly gulp and my legs threaten to give out. "I'm not doing this today."

She looks honest-to-God nervous, but also determined, and that shit is scary. "Tell me what happened to you. I can guess, but I need to hear it."

No. No. No. Not happening.

I can't do this. I feel like the walls of the bathroom are about to swallow me whole. "No."

She drops her shoulders, looking down at the floor. But Blair doesn't stay defeated for long. Her chin lifts, and she looks at me with so much empathy I want to vomit again. She shouldn't feel for me. "Do you talk about it in meetings?"

"Fuck no."

"Did you in rehab?"

I walk out of the bathroom into the bedroom, but she follows, and I give up to turn and face her. "No."

"Well, no fucking wonder you can't cope, Rhys."

I lean in close to her, looking into those eyes that tell me how much she fucking cares about me even if she doesn't want to. "I'm coping fine."

She scoffs. "Tell me what happened to you at that last foster home. What the hell are you so afraid of?"

"Everything!" I raise my arms in the air as I plead with her not to do this. I drop my arms to my sides, my own shoulders slouching. "Everyone sees me as this tough, strong man. Muscles. Tattoos. Quiet." I sink down to her bed, sitting on the edge. "But on the inside, I'm quaking with fear all of the time. I'm a scrawny, dirty, hundred-pound kid, shaking and puking at the thought of being touched."

I look up at her and see she's walked closer to me, standing before me. "Why? Please just tell me why."

"No."

She moves to her knees before me, looking up at me now. "I see you as a strong man, Rhys." Her hand rests on the bed next to my thigh. "But I've always been able to see that little boy inside too."

I feel bile rising in my throat, hating that kid. "Why are you always trying to help me?"

"You think I don't have a little girl inside of me? That this badass, bitchy persona isn't just a front?"

"I know it is."

She smiles with determination and confidence. "Exactly. You see me, Rhys. And I hate it most of the time, but I also love it too. Somehow you see me, and you make me see me too."

I know she's all good. She has been since the first night when I couldn't fuck her, and she didn't make me feel like a freak. She came back for more.

"Tell me, Rhys."

I shake my head slowly from side to side. "No."

"Rhys." Her voice is begging, a strangled cry as she pleads for me to divulge my deepest of secrets.

"We have to go."

She shakes her head emphatically. "You can't go like this into our marriage. You have to tell me. Get rid of these demons so we can move forward."

"I'm the fucking demon." I stand up, and she stands with me, denying it with a shake of her head. But I grab her chin with my hand gently, making her look at me. "I am. I fucked my foster mother." I feel the shame and horror creeping up through me, but I need her to drop this shit. "And I liked it. From fourteen to fifteen, for almost a year and a half, I fucked her."

I release her, and she watches me with caution but not disgust. "That's not it." Mother. Fucker. She is a pain. "There's more to it. I know there is."

"God damn it, Blair. We have to go."

"No." She places a hand over her chest as it rises and falls. She looks sick. "That's not why you flinch when I touch you. That's not why you can't kiss me. And I say 'can't' because I see you look at my lips and I know you want to."

I stare at her lips now, full and painted pink. And God she's right. I would love to feel what it's like to kiss the ever-loving fuck out of her, to taste her mouth and let my tongue take over instead of my fucked-up mind. But I know I'd scare her when I would freak the fuck out.

I pry my gaze from her lips and move toward the door. "Let's go."

"Rhys, tell me. Tell me why you can't stand to look at me when we fuck. That's not why."

I march back over to her, fury flying through me as I clench my teeth and will my body to calm down. "Don't fucking talk about it anymore. I don't want to talk about it. Let's go. Now."

And this time, her shoulders slouch and stay that way as we grab Bree and pile into the car.

On the way to our wedding from hell.

Blair

WE STAND in front of the judge and exchange generic vows as I watch the man about to become my husband.

I know he's tortured. I know there's so much more to his backstory, and for whatever reason, I thought he'd tell me before we got married.

It was naïve to think that. It was stupid to believe he'd want to do that when this marriage is only on paper, but I wanted to know.

I want to take the pain away, even if it's only slightly.

"By the power vested in me by the state of Missouri, I now pronounce you 'man and wife'." The judge finishes and tells us we can kiss, but I shake my head, just asking him to sign the paper.

Rhys won't kiss me.

We take Bree to school three hours late, but we made sure her absence was excused this morning, and then we part ways. Our wedding day is spent in separate parts of the city, working. After work, everything is normal for us.

I pick Bree up at Rhys's shop. We go home. I order dinner, and then Rhys comes home at night. Nothing has changed. We didn't even exchange rings, although I know we need to get them for the show we'll need to put on.

We all hang out, watching television, and then Bree heads to bed.

I pick up the living room and then turn to Rhys who is still on the couch, looking so fucking numb I think I could stab him in the leg and he wouldn't feel it.

"I'm going to bed."

He nods with barely even a grunt as I climb the stairs and go up to my room. I strip out of my dress and stand naked for a moment, looking into the floor length mirror near my dresser.

"What exactly are you looking at?"

I turn around and see Rhys in the doorway as I stand there naked. There are so many things I want to say, but I don't. Somehow, I feel conquered tonight and just want to crawl in my bed, but I know I'm supposed to wear clothes now, so I pull open the pajama drawer in my dresser.

I hear the door click closed, and I feel him behind me before I can decide what to wear. "I'm sorry."

I turn around to look up at him. "What?"

"Blair." He looks so fucking tormented. "I'm sorry for such a shitty wedding."

"It wasn't that bad." My voice is quiet as I look up at him.

"It was." He slowly drags the back of his hand over my bare arm, sending shivers through my entire body, making the fine, blond hairs on my arms stand up. "I hate thinking about that house."

I want him to talk to me so badly, but I know I can't force him. "Maybe telling me, actually saying it out loud will help somehow."

"I want it buried."

I ache to touch him, but I don't. His hand drifts over the skin on my stomach, just barely grazing me. "It's not though, Rhys. It's alive in you."

I watch his Adam's apple bob in his throat with his own agony, and I feel it inside. "I wasn't lying. I fucked her."

I had a feeling that part wasn't a lie. "Okay."

His eyes snap up to mine. "Doesn't that disgust you?"

"Did you want to?" I hate asking these questions. I hate forcing him to talk, but I know it's the only way to free him. I can feel his shame.

His head shakes side to side as he drops his hand, and I yearn for his touch to return. "When I first moved in with the Bradfords, everyone thought I was so fucking lucky. I was fourteen, and they chose me to live with them. Scrawny little street kid with dirt under his fingernails in their great big mansion." I try to show no emotion. "But then a week went by and I began to see just how unlucky I was. Mr. Bradford would get extremely fucking drunk and beat the living shit out of me. They had three kids of their own, all younger than me, prized possessions and, as far as I know, he never touched them."

He takes his shirt off, unbuttoning it slowly and letting it drop to the floor as he takes more steps back away from me.

"I don't have any scars. None. My body is flawless on the outside, but to me it's fucking ugly."

I scan every carved muscle, every dip and ridge before meeting his eyes. "You're anything, but ugly." He's painfully beautiful, but I know it's the scars on the inside that torture him.

"A couple months in, I woke up in the middle of the night thinking I was having a wet dream or something, but when I pushed the cover down, I saw it was a living nightmare. Mrs. Bradford with my cock in her mouth."

"So, you didn't want it."

He undoes the button on his jeans. "I came down her throat."

"That doesn't matter. That's biology. Someone sucks on your dick, you come." I feel defensive for him. I hate that he thinks he asked for it.

His jaw ticks as he pushes his jeans down and off, leaving him naked as well as me. Both of us vulnerable and bare to one another. "Soon I started waking up to her riding me, assuring me it was okay, that her husband didn't care and she was on birth control so I could come inside her."

I try not to vomit, thinking about this bitch acting like they were in a relationship when, in fact, she was a predator. She was supposed to protect him.

"I'm sorry, Rhys."

"Don't. Don't do that."

I shoot him a questioning glance. "Don't do what?"

"Don't pity me. I was fourteen. I could have told someone. I didn't."

"You were a kid. In their care."

He walks to me, standing before me, this magnificent, gorgeous man. "Four months in, it wasn't just us in my room." My eyes widen, and he's in a numb state again, looking right through me. "He would watch. And then beat the living shit out of me after I came. If she came too, he'd beat me more."

I clutch my throat, my body reacting no matter how hard I try not to. I want to weep for him, but I keep the sobs at bay.

"Six months in, it wasn't just her fucking me."

I feel tears sting my eyes. "Rhys . . ." It's a weak gasp.

"I thought he was just going to watch again." His eyes close, and words can't describe the pain radiating from him and going directly to my heart. "But he fucked me. For almost a full year. And I let them. I was small and weak from years of malnutrition and barely enough food to live when I lived with them, despite their wealth."

His eyes open and scan my face as I struggle not to let the sobs wrack my body.

"They made it feel good, Blair. I came, every fucking time. My dick was hard for them."

I shake my head from side to side. "That doesn't mean you wanted it. And then he beat you. It's all abuse, Rhys."

He shrugs his large shoulder. His body bare, but for the first time, I don't want to look anywhere except into his eyes.

"You didn't deserve that."

He laughs without an ounce of humor. "I was their fuckdoll. And when I was good, they bought me shit. Although they didn't want to feed me much so I'd stay weak. I'd shove my face full at school and use their gym until finally, I added muscle."

That's why he works out so often, why he stays muscular. "That's why you don't like to be touched."

"I'm fucked-up, Blair. Damaged. They made sex feel good when I didn't want it, so I grew to despise sex. When I finally got big enough to fight back, I beat the shit out of Mr. Bradford and I threatened them both that if they came after me, I'd slit their throats in their sleep."

Good.

"I ran, and they didn't report it. I found a shitty apartment, and I tried my best to forget about them. I dated Quinn. I tried not to be a nervous wreck, but the first time I kissed her, I felt so fucking sick like I was going to puke that I numbed myself with anything I could get my hands on."

"I don't blame you for not wanting to remember."

I go to him, keeping a small distance between our naked bodies. "So, you haven't kissed anyone since?"

"Not that I remember. I had to be drugged or drunk out of my mind before I could get my dick to work. I barely remember any sexual experiences after that."

I hate that he's missed out on so many things because of what those sick motherfuckers did to him. "Rhys . . . you're not damaged. They are."

"I'm pretty fucking damaged, Blair." He looks down at my body. "Look at you. You're fucking beautiful, and when we have sex I rush as fast as I can to get off because I just want it to be over."

The admission guts me even if I already knew that. "So, don't."

He looks at me, confused and angry. "Don't?"

"Don't rush. Don't pull away from me. I'm not them."

"It doesn't fucking matter. I close my eyes, and I smell her fucking expensive, gag-inducing perfume. I feel his cock pressing into me." I cry for him, and he keeps going. "I feel his fists slamming into my face. Her hands and mouth on my dick that swelled for her."

I shake my head, tears falling. "You got hard because you were fourteen and someone was touching your cock. It wasn't because you wanted it or even because it felt good."

I see his eyes filling with hot, angry tears, and I want to scream.

Fuck every adult who ever hurt a child, who robbed them of their innocence. "Rhys. Look at me."

He doesn't.

His head hangs down, and I do the only thing I can do to try to bring him back to me.

I touch him.

Rhys

I JOLT to life when I feel her hand on my bare stomach, the muscles tighten as my hand grabs her wrist to pull her away.

"Rhys. It's me."

I look into her eyes. "I know who you are."

She shakes her head, tears spilling down her cheeks. I wasn't even sure she was capable of crying, but hey, my fucked-up reality would make anyone sob.

I've never, ever spelled out the abuse I suffered at the hands of the Bradfords. I got drunk one time and told Quinn in a slurred mess of words I'm not even sure she could decipher, but I've never talked about it sober and with so much clarity.

But Blair needs to know who she married.

She needs to know just how fucked-up I am because right now as her fingers touch my skin, I feel sick to the point of throwing up.

Because sex is confusing to me. They made it feel so good I had an orgasm, but inside I felt like I was going to die, like I wanted to die.

I don't let go of her wrist, but she flattens her palm over my abs and slides it up over my heart with my hand still latched onto her. "Thank you for telling me. I know that's probably only the surface . . ."

"No that's it. They both fucked me, and he beat me for two years."

"You're generalizing it."

"You want more details?" I glare down at her, but she doesn't back down now.

"No," she shakes her head, "unless you need to talk about it. But everything they did was wrong, no matter how good they made it feel. It was wrong."

"I know that," I snap.

"Do you think I'm going to see you differently?"

"Ha," I laugh coldly. "Don't you?"

"No. I already knew who you were, but now that I understand why you flinch when I touch you . . ." Her hand drags down over my ab muscles again, my hand still around her wrist. "Now, maybe I can help you get through it."

"How?" I'm so fucking angry I could scream. I know this is Blair's hand in mine. Not either of the Bradfords', but it doesn't matter. I still feel repulsed by the touch.

"Do you trust me, Rhys?"

I look at her, really look into her eyes, searching the depths of her soul. But I shake my head. "I don't trust anyone."

Her lips lift with a small smile I don't expect. "I think you do. I think you trust me."

Her hand smooths over my lower stomach, and I fight the urge to jerk away.

"I've been used before, Rhys. My whole life I was a toy, a warm body for men to do what they wanted with it and then throw away." I feel sick knowing that's definitely the truth and that I'm one of those worthless motherfuckers. "But you're the only one who makes me feel useful." I'm surprised by that. "Like I helped you in some way."

"You did."

She smiles sweetly, almost too sweetly for Blair, but I don't point it out. "So, let me help you."

"I freak out, Blair. Touch is just . . ." Disgusting. I think it, but it's like she filled it in.

"Not mine." She takes her other hand and brushes it over my cheek, and I feel like I'm going to leap out of my skin, but I stay put. "I think whether you wanted to or not, you kind of like me."

"I do." I close my eyes. "But it doesn't matter. It's not you, Blair."

"Shhh . . ." What the fuck? I open my eyes just as her lips approach mine, but don't touch. "Did you ever kiss her?"

"No. Fuck no. She was always slobbering all over me, but I would rather cut out my tongue than kiss her back." I force my eyes closed again, trying to will away the memories of her acting like she was making love to me. Like I wanted it. Her lips all over mine. Her tongue in my mouth. Mr. Bradford was all about control and showing me who was in charge. For her it was some sick fantasy. And I don't know which one was worse.

"Rhys . . . Come back to me." I feel her breath on my lips, smell her sweet breath that smells like the strawberry ice cream we had after dinner.

"Blair, don't do this. I don't want to hurt you when I freak the fuck out. Because I will."

I can feel her desire to fix me and only feel guilt because I know she can't. No one can.

"Kiss me." My eyes snap open as I stare down at her.

"What? I just said I don't kiss."

"You said you didn't kiss her, but this is me. Blair." Her free hand rests on my shoulder, and I wince at the touch. "Kiss me because you want to, and I know you do."

God, I do. I look down at her lips and swallow the need to touch my lips to them. "I can't."

"You can. I want you to. You want to. Take your power back, Rhys."

"You mean my balls?"

She looks down between our bodies, straight at my junk and then up at me. "You definitely still have your balls."

Oddly enough, just that simple glance stirs my dick to life even though we've been talking naked for several minutes now. "I've never kissed anyone sober without freaking out."

"So kiss me, and we'll see."

"You act like it's so fucking easy."

Her lips ghost over mine, hovering there, but allowing me to have the control. "It is."

I urge her to move back until her back is pressed against the wall. I want the control. I want to fucking kiss her without running away and throwing up. But I don't know if I'm capable of that, no matter how easy she thinks it is.

I take both of her wrists now and pull her arms up, pinning them to the wall. But I don't release them, I cling to them.

"You can't fix me."

"I don't want to. You're exactly who I want you to be."

I search her eyes, waiting for her to laugh at me or call me a freak. Something. But she doesn't. She just tilts her chin up, her hands lax in mine, letting me have the power.

My heart is jackhammering in my chest. But I push through because I want this, and I'll be damned if I let them take this from me even if it's only one kiss.

I press my mouth against hers tentatively at first before she whimpers softly against my lips, and I lose it. I kiss her with everything I have, and she parts her lips, allowing my tongue to sweep in, lashing against hers. I taste her sweet mouth as she nips on my bottom lip, pulling it between her teeth and then kissing my lips passionately like she wants to devour me, like she can expel all of my demons with her mouth, and I want to let her. I feel her breast pressing against my chest, feel her panting with need as my now rock-solid cock presses against her stomach.

"God, Rhys," she gasps, and I want so badly to fuck her against the wall, but then it happens.

The memories of what we talked about, of that fucking delusional succubus dragging her lips all over my body, of her straddling my lap and insisting on eye contact while she rode me. And I push back.

I'm panting for an entirely different reason as I move back and sit on the chair I normally sleep on, my fingers threading through my hair and threatening to pull the strands from my head.

I'm such a fucking freak.

She looks terrified as she walks over to me about to place her hands on my shoulders, but I yank back. "Don't."

She nods. "Okay."

"It's not you, Blair. You're gorgeous." I look up at her naked body, my eyes drifting over all her tan, smooth skin. "I want to fuck you. I want to so fucking badly, but my mind..."

"Shhh." She doesn't touch me now, but her eyes have me locked in a hold as she peers down at me, cowering on the chair. "I want you to fuck me too." Her hand slides over her flat stomach. "That kiss was so fucking hot."

I watch her hand as it dips lower and look up at her, raising an eyebrow. "What are you doing?"

"We're married now, Rhys. For better and worse and all that. We're going to have to figure out how to have sex."

I'm irrationally angry now, which of course turns me into an asshole. "If you need it that fucking bad, I'm sure you can find a dick to ride."

She looks at me, burying the hurt and trudging forward because that's Blair. "I don't want just any dick." Her eyes move to my lap where my cock is still up and ready, even if my mind is fucked. "I want yours. My husband's. On our wedding night."

It isn't just about sex. I can see it in her eyes. She needs this. She wants to heal me even if I don't deserve it. Even if she'll fail. And she will fail.

"I had a panic attack from a kiss." My heart is still beating far too fast in my chest.

"So, we'll work into this slowly." She turns away from me, but she doesn't move. "Do you want me, Rhys?"

She can't see me, but I nod my head. My voice is strained with anxiety and desire. "Yes."

She moves to sit on my lap, facing away from me. "So, baby steps. If it's too much, we stop. No matter what we're doing, but sex is supposed to feel good. And you should want it. If you don't have both parts of the equation, then it's not sex. It's betrayal. It's abuse. It's rape."

I flinch at her words, but I know she's right. And holy fuck, do I want this as she guides my cock between her legs and I slide inside of her. "You'll get tired of this, Blair." I whisper in her ear and feel her body shudder as she moves her hips, guiding my cock further into her.

"How could I tire of this?"

I let my hands travel forward and cup her bare breasts, pinching her nipples and letting myself enjoy her moans.

"I may never be able to kiss you again."

She's panting as she rides me reverse cowgirl style, and I squeeze her tits in my hands. "You will. It was too good not to do it again."

"Right. When I freaked out."

Her head leans back into my chest as she uses her hands as leverage against the chair, riding me and bringing us both toward release.

"I'm not afraid of you, Rhys. I want every part of you."

I try to tell myself she's lost in ecstasy, but I know she means it. One of my hands dips lower, finding her clit and making slow circles coaxing her orgasm from her.

"Rhys," she moans my name, and I close my eyes, breathing her in, reminding me exactly who I'm fucking.

"You're in trouble, Blair. I'll crush you."

"Or I'll heal you."

I hope she's right. I want her to be right so fucking badly.

"I'm damaged beyond repair."

"Come with me, Rhys." Her voice is higher as she approaches her orgasm, and I feel the rush bubbling up through my entire body as I rub her clit and hold her breast with my other hand, pulling her back against my chest, wanting to feel her. "If we break, we'll do it together, and then we'll pick up the pieces."

I moan near her ear, and she rocks against me, coming around my cock as I come deep inside her, allowing one moment of freedom from everything else.

But an overwhelming fear washes over me once it's over because what if it never happens like this again?

Rhys

I'M NAKED and laying flat on my back on the king-sized bed. I should have moved to the chair I've been sleeping on hours ago because I've slept maybe a couple of hours all night, scrunched to the edge of the bed, nearly falling off.

Because I'm incredibly fucked-up. After we both finished with Blair on my lap last night, she asked me to come to bed. And after my wife—paper or not—my legal wife, told me she wouldn't touch me while we slept, I reluctantly agreed.

And now, she's naked and asleep on her side of the bed. She put a line of fluffy pillows between us to assure me that we wouldn't touch.

I swivel my head to look over at her across the pillow barrier. The covers are pulled over most of her body, but I can see the hint of her right nipple peeking out. God, she's beautiful.

She's everything I don't deserve.

I've done so many fucked-up things in my short life. I'm certain I'll do more. And to top it all off, a normal man would be all over her naked body this morning after seeing she's still naked from last night. But me?

I'm trying to keep my breathing under control because last night was a lot to handle, telling her my secrets, kissing her, wanting so badly to let her touch me.

NICOLE DYKES

The few times I briefly slept last night were full of hellish memories, and I'm so fucking pissed-off about everything. Angry when I should feel fully satisfied.

I look away from Blair's sleeping body, feeling the shame from trapping her with a damaged man.

"Um . . . Rhys?"

Oh shit. I pull the covers up higher, well above my waist as Bree walks into our bedroom hesitantly. Blair must hear her too, and she sits up, thankfully pulling the covers up to her chin.

"What's up, Bree?" I try to keep my voice casual, but of course, it's not.

She's looking up at the ceiling and not at us, thank God. "Is someone going to take me to school?"

I glance over at the clock. "Shit. Yeah. I'll be down in a minute."

She nods and then leaves the room. I jump out of the bed, but Blair is laughing now as she lets the sheet drop, almost making me groan at the site of her naked chest. "Well, I think we're officially parents. Our kid just walked in on us post-fuck."

I tug on a pair of jeans and try to pry my eyes off her. "We're a good eight hours post-fuck."

She nods her head and then raises her hands in the air, using the tie around her wrist to secure her hair in a ponytail, but my eyes are on her raised tits. What the hell is wrong with me?

I just had sex last night, and now I want her again? Why am I this desperate to possibly humiliate myself with another panic attack?

I pull a shirt on over my head. "I'll see ya tonight."

"Wait."

I look over at her, hoping she doesn't want to talk anymore about the shit that went down with the Bradfords because I'm barely hanging on by a thread as it is. "What?"

"Do you want me to grab you a ring when I get mine today?"

A ring? "A wedding ring?"

She rolls her eyes as she climbs out of the bed, slipping into a robe she doesn't tie. "Yes. We're married, remember?"

"I thought it was just for show." I'm a prick. I know that by the slight pout on her lips.

"Yeah it is." She fastens the silky tie across her waist and takes a seat on the bed. "But don't you think we should show them wedding bands."

She's thought of everything, and I'm, of course, just being a dick. She's showing her sweet side that I actually like because it still has her spin on it, but I'll always be a surly motherfucker. "I'll get your ring, okay?"

Her right eyebrow shoots up. "You will?"

"Yeah, I will. It won't be anything like you would have probably expected, but I'll get you a ring."

She rolls her eyes and lies back on the bed, making the already short robe ride up her thighs. "First of all, fuck you," she laughs and turns her head toward me. "Second of all, I can't wait."

"Good." I look nervously out the door and then back to Blair. "I'm going to approach the whole private school thing with her."

She sits up again, looking confused. "What private school thing?"

"Blair, we have to look good on paper, remember? The Herringtons could and would give her the best education. If we are going toe-to-toe with them, we need to be ready."

She's thinking it over, and I can tell she's as worried as I feel about it because Bree isn't going to like it. "She's going to be pissed."

I nod, already knowing that. "I know she will, but we have to do everything we can to keep her safe, right?"

"Yes." She says it with a definitive tone, and I have to admit I love the mama bear side of her.

Normal husband—kisses his gorgeous, sexy wife goodbye.

Rhys—grunts a goodbye and leaves.

When I get downstairs, Bree is waiting by the door. "I'm going to be late."

I grab my keys from the side table. "Then let's go."

She follows me out to the car, and we're both quiet as usual. As we approach the school, I've finally talked myself into talking to her about private school. "Bree, I have to talk to you about something..."

"I'm sorry. I should have knocked harder."

She knocked? Fuck, I must have been more out of it than I thought. "No. Not that. We should have locked the door before we..." She looks horrified, and I finally shut the fuck up. "Sorry." I shake it off. "No. I need to talk to you about private school."

Her gaze darkens as it meets mine in the rearview, and we creep ahead in the school's drop-off line. "What about private school?"

Just say it, Rhys. "I think we might need to enroll you in one."

"What?" She's panicked. "No. I don't want to go to private school. I like my school."

I nod toward the front entrance. "They have metal detectors at the door."

"They're keeping us safe." She folds her small arms over her chest and glares. "I don't want to go to a private school. My friends are here."

"I know."

"They were going to make me go to a fancy private school, Rhys. You aren't them."

I cringe, thinking about any sort of comparison between me and that motherfucker, Mr. Herrington. "I'm not, but that's the point. He can tell the judge that he can give you everything I can't."

I hate that I can see tears glistening in her eyes from here. I'm a total asshole for doing this to her before school, and I contemplate getting out of line and taking her for ice cream or some shit.

"I don't care about that kind of stuff."

"I know you don't, Bree." I grip the steering wheel, feeling nothing but tension. "I don't either, but the judge will. We have to do whatever we can so Blair and I look like the better parents."

She shakes her head, anger and sadness mixing as she looks at me when I park the car as the next one to drop off a student. "Don't do this to me."

Fuck, my heart actually hurts. "I'm sorry."

She shoves the door open and climbs out, slamming the door,

not saying another word to me. And, of fucking course, both of the little punks she hangs out with are instantly on it, already knowing she's pissed about something as she approaches them.

I don't want to leave her, but I follow the line out and go to work.

I'm doing fucking great at this parenting thing already.

Blair

I TUG OPEN the glass door of Rhys's shop and see him sitting behind the front desk, his feet propped up. "So, this is what you do all day?"

He drops his feet to the floor. "Mostly."

I don't believe him, but I do like giving him a hard time. I didn't want him to leave this morning and feel slightly pathetic, knowing the reason I'm here can wait until tonight, but I wanted to see him.

"Shouldn't you be at work?"

I shrug my shoulders and walk behind the desk. "I'm tired of work. I thought we could play." I give him the naughtiest of smiles and wag my eyebrows, being over-the-top ridiculous, but I see the fear in his eyes.

"Blair..."

I knock off the shit and shake my head. "I'm kidding."

He doesn't look like he believes me. "I know that last night we—"

"Had sex. Hot sex." I finish for him. "And it wasn't the first time."

I watch him swallow hard as his eyes land on mine, looking so fucking tortured and tired. "I know, but... the kiss and everything."

"I know, Rhys." I don't want him to be hurting because I forced him to talk. "I was just fucking around."

"I know, but also you aren't, right? And you deserve a normal guy who can fuck you whenever you want it and can kiss you goodbye."

I can't stand him thinking I deserve anything other than him. "Rhys..." I move to only a couple of inches away from him. "You aren't getting rid of me, so there will be no goodbyes and," the intensity in his gaze nearly sets me on fire, but I keep pushing, "we will kiss again."

I want to touch him, stroke his cheek, but I don't. He's feeling vulnerable today. "And if I can't?"

"You can. You will. When you want to, you have my permission to kiss the fuck out of me."

That pulls his lips into a smirk that melts my heart. I thought was made of ice. "I will."

It's firm, and I like it. "I'm not actually here to fuck you."

"No?"

I shake my head. "Nope. I called Bree's twat caseworker today to talk about the private school thing."

"And?"

"And we can send her to a private school as long as we pay for it." I leave out the part about her giving me attitude, but it's not important.

"How much is it?" He looks worried, and I know the worry is only going to grow.

"I called today, and it'll be about twenty grand." His eyes bulge, but I try my best to downplay it. "And even though it already started, as long as we pay in full, they'll let her start in a week."

"Twenty grand?"

"I have it covered."

"No," he growls, pushing his fingers through his hair, and I know he's worked up. "It was my idea, all of it."

"Stop." I know I'm a spoiled brat, and the only money I have is because of my father, but I want him to understand I'm in this with him. "Rhys, I want to. Bree isn't just your responsibility." I hold up a hand to silence the argument I already knew was coming. "No matter what I said at the beginning. I'm in this. We're adopting her, and I have a trust fund just sitting there. We have a meeting with the school tomorrow."

"What? That fast?"

"The sooner the better." I sigh. "The caseworker also let me know we have seventy-two days until the hearing. So, it's even less than the three months Gillian thought. We need to get moving."

Yup, he's even more stressed now. The muscles in his arm are flexed tight as he messes with his hair, and I want to drop to my knees and try my best to relieve some tension, but I know, with Rhys, that would only add to it.

I have to rewire my way of thinking to navigate around what those abusive fuckers did to him, but for him, I'm more than happy to do it.

"She was so pissed-off this morning, slammed the car door and everything."

I almost laugh. I knew she was going to give him hell. "Yeah well, we're about to adopt a kid that's almost a teenage girl. You might as well get used to that right now."

He looks so sad. "She almost cried when I told her, Blair. She doesn't cry."

I know she's going to be upset, and I hate the idea of her crying. She's a little Rhys. "I know, but we have to go for it, like you said. Make ourselves look as good as we can, and then once she's ours, we'll make it right."

"She's going to hate us."

"She'll be okay." I look down at his lap, unable to help myself and then back to his mouth, that sexy, ever present pout, and bite my bottom lip. "Okay, so now back to the fucking."

"Blair." It's a warning growl that I ignore.

"I can't stop thinking about last night and your lips. God, I love your lips, so sexy and full. Kind of like kissing a girl."

"I'm not sure that's a compliment."

I shrug my shoulders. "It was hot."

"I can't . . ." He's choked up, and I almost lose my confidence because the last thing I want is to cause him pain.

"Relax. I meant what I said . . . the next kiss is on you, when you want it. I'm not going to kiss you, Rhys." I turn my back to him and sit on his lap, straddling him as I face away. "But I am going to fuck you."

I start to grind over his lap and feel him stirring beneath me as I smile with satisfaction. "Blair, this is my shop."

"Which makes it so much hotter." I take hold of his hand, noticing his instant recoil, but I don't let him jerk away from me. Instead I move his hand under my skirt. There's a large glass window and a glass door at the front, not shielding us, but the desk does a good job of hiding what's going on under the waist.

"I'm already wet for you."

His groan sends satisfaction through me as his fingers slide through my folds, and I shamelessly grind against his hand. "Fuck, Blair. You aren't wearing panties."

"Why would I? I knew I was coming to see you."

His moan behind me only makes me hotter. I release his hand, leaving him under my skirt while he finds my clit, pulling a gasp from me before I find the button and zipper of his jeans. It's an awkward angle, but I manage, already feeling how hard he is for me.

"Fuck me, Rhys."

He doesn't fight me, just removes his hand from my skirt before using one arm to hold me around my waist while lifting us both up and forcing his jeans down to free himself. I waste no time moving back, spreading my legs and taking him inside me as I lean my front against the desk. "God, Rhys . . ."

I moan as he fills me and roll my hips as he thrusts inside. "Fuck, Blair," he groans, and I'm already close, having been already so worked up before he pushed into me.

I keep my eyes on the front of the store, just in case there's an approaching customer, but he makes it hard as he pushes his massive dick to the hilt, stretching my pussy around him. "God, I love when you fill me with your big cock. Don't stop."

But he stills, making me whimper from the loss of the movement. "Don't say that, okay?"

What? I try not to get upset. He doesn't sound angry, more devastated. "I'm sorry."

He pulls back, his dick nearly all the way out, and I think he's going to make me stop, but instead he thrusts forward, filling me again, pulling a long moan from my mouth. "Don't be sorry." I feel his breath on the back of my neck, and I'm glad I put my hair up today. "You feel so fucking good."

His voice is all gravel and want, sending pleasure through my entire body. "Oh God, Rhys. Don't stop."

His hands grip my hips as he guides me over his cock, moving us both toward release that we both need.

I'm never going to stop trying with him, no matter the consequences. I will help him heal even if it takes a piece of me to do it.

Rhys

I can feel how nervous and angry Bree is as she stands by my side with Blair looking up at the fancy prep school before us.

Bree gave both of us the silent treatment last night and this morning. And I get it. I'd be fucking pissed too if someone tried to shove me in an uppity school like this one.

The Bradfords didn't do that to me, but I suspect it was because more questions would be asked at a small private school, especially when I was usually covered in bruises. The public school I went to probably chalked it up to me fighting. Which I did.

"Please don't do this." Big blue eyes look up at me, and I almost relent. But Blair speaks before I can run away with Bree.

"It won't be so bad, Bree. I promise you, okay? The worst that's going to happen is you get to school some douchey rich kids."

"I don't want to go to school with a bunch of rich jerks."

Fuck. How can I make her do this?

"Hey, I went to a private school," Blair says with a teasing smile, setting Bree up on purpose.

Bree scoffs, rolling her eyes and takes the easy bait. "My point."

Blair laughs, and Bree gives her own version of a smile. I shake my head at them both but enjoy watching them. I kneel down in front of Bree, trying to get her attention. "Bree, we need this. You only have to go until we're in the clear, until after the hearing." Even if throwing away the rest of the twenty grand I still don't want Blair to pony up will probably kill me. If she doesn't want this and she's legally ours, I'll let her walk away the second she's safe.

"You swear?"

My head swivels to Blair for confirmation because apparently, I do that now. She nods with a smile, and I focus back on Bree. "I promise."

She huffs, clearly not happy as she folds her arms over her chest. "Fine. But can I ask you for something?" She looks down at the ground, looking slightly guilty as she adds, "I mean, something else."

"You can ask us for anything," Blair quickly reacts to her shameful appearance. "Don't ever hold back from us."

I nod in agreement as I stand back up, a little nervous about what she's going to ask for.

"Okay . . . um, my birthday is this weekend." Fuuuuuck. How did I not know that? "And I was wondering if maybe . . . Fletch and Rhett could stay over?"

Blair's already nodding her head yes as I'm shaking my head no. "Like, stay the night? No."

Blair shoots me an irritated look. "Rhys. It's her birthday."

"So I should let her have two boys stay the night?"

"Not boys, my best friends." Bree is upset, but I'm not letting two little dipshits with dicks sleep over.

"No." I shake my head again, clearly freaked the fuck out.

Blair rolls her eyes. "She's turning twelve. The boys are also twelve?" Blair looks to Bree for confirmation.

"Fletcher is twelve. Rhett's thirteen."

"No." I shake my head again. And I know it's being completely ignored by Blair.

"Yes. Of course you can. You guys can sleep down in the living room." Blair overrides me, and Bree smiles.

I look at Blair. "Blair . . . no boys. How will that look to the judge if someone says anything?"

"We aren't hosting an orgy, Rhys." She smiles down at Bree, who looks slightly nervous, but not too bad. She knows who wears the pants, and it's annoying the shit out of me. "She's having her two best friends over for her birthday party, eating pizza and watching movies like any preteen does for her birthday."

She's pleading with me to shut the fuck up, but I can't help it. These boys are right in the throes of puberty, and they'll be sleeping in a room with Bree.

Bree looks cautiously up at me. "I don't like it. They're still boys."

Bree shrugs her shoulders. "They can't help that they have penises, Rhys."

Fuck, Me. I stare at her, horrified as Blair cackles uncontrollably. "Oh, so true," she says in between cracking up.

"It's not funny. They're going to want to use them soon, Bree."

She scrunches up her nose at me, like I'm the one who took it too far. "Ew."

"Exactly," I say, and Blair and she both give me the exact same look. Like I'm overreacting.

"Bree." Blair holds her chin affectionately in her hand, looking down at her. "You can have them over for your birthday. No kissing."

"Gross," Bree says, pulling another laugh from Blair as she releases her and turns to me.

"You, the dad thing, is super hot, but you need to chill."

I roll my eyes, and we hear another "Gross" from Bree as I give in for now at least.

"Fine. Let's just talk about it later. Right now, we have to go meet this douche."

"Great attitude, Rhys," Blair lectures, but she's wearing a grin and also looks like she wants to mount me right here.

And after yesterday in my shop and the night before, my body starts to react to her before I clear my throat and direct them both toward the school.

We head toward the office and meet with the pretentious motherfucker in a suit who looks over Bree and says she will be a good fit once she's in the official school uniform.

Bree looks like she's going to puke, and I feel the same, but Blair shines in these moments. She has a way of covering up her disdain for people while still letting them have it with subtle jabs.

We enroll her, and Blair hands over a twenty-thousand-dollar check before we walk out of the school that will be Bree's for at least a few months.

Bree sulks the whole drive home, and I hate that I feel like I've let her down already. But I keep telling myself it will all be worth it.

"Okay, you can have them both stay the night Saturday for your birthday, and I won't complain much."

Blair smiles over at me, and Bree at least drops the angry face, moving to a more indifferent look.

"Thanks."

"It will be fine, Rhys," Blair assures me.

But I still don't fucking like it.

Blair

BREE IS STARTING at the private school next week and is not happy about it. So, I've decided to make her party as good as I possibly can. It was hilarious to see Rhys all worked up about her having boys stay over, but I'm pretty sure to Bree, they aren't boys.

They are her comfort. Her constant.

And I'm determined to make them feel welcome. I walk into the front door, my arms completely full as Rhys and Bree both meet me at the door. Bree's eyes widen. "Whoa, what is all of this?"

I eye her and see she's completely serious. I hand Rhys the cake I picked up at the bakery and hand her some balloons while holding on to the presents I managed to grab. "It's all for your birthday, silly."

Rhys and Bree share a look before Rhys shrugs and walks into the kitchen with the cake. I look at Bree. "I have more out in the car. When will Fletcher and Rhett be here?"

"Should be soon." She's looking at the presents as I place them on the coffee table. "You guys didn't have to do this. I just wanted them to be able to hang out."

She reminds me so much of Rhys sometimes, uncertain when someone is being nice, always waiting for the other shoe to drop. "And they are totally going to, but I want this birthday and all your birthdays to be special, Bree."

I see Rhys walk back into the living room out of the corner of my eye, but he doesn't approach us. He just stands at a distance with his arms folded and watching us. "Why?"

I don't glance over at Rhys, even if I'm pretty sure he could shed some light on the confusion I'm feeling right now. "Why wouldn't I want you to have a good birthday?"

"I don't know, Blair. It's just weird. I remember one birthday with my mom out of twelve, and she didn't seem to care about it."

My heart aches for her, and I feel so shitty because I spent so much time feeling sorry for myself because my dad was always too busy for me, but even he bought me a damn cake for my birthday. "Well, that changes now. We'll make sure you love every birthday from now on."

She only offers a small smile, but I see the sad uncertainty in it.

"What's wrong, Bree?"

Her shoulders shrug. "That's only if you guys win custody, right?"

I brush that off easily. "There's no way we won't, Bree. You can't think like that." I wrap my arms around her, not giving her a choice as I hug her to my body because I want her to feel safe. I need it.

She stiffens, but she accepts the hug, patting me on the back. I release her but use my hands to smooth down her unruly hair, and she swipes me away, laughing.

"I'm going to get the rest of the presents out of the car." She nods her head.

As I start toward the door, I can feel Rhys coming with me. When we reach the car, he helps me gather the rest of the presents. I guess I went a little overboard, but he doesn't say anything about it.

"You really sure about this?" He looks so nervous, and I find it cute. Nervous is not a way I can often describe Rhys.

"Yes. I'm sure. They're her best friends. Think about you, Sean, Logan, and Quinn."

He looks pained as he glances toward the house and then back to me. "Logan and I both fucked Quinn."

The hot streak of jealousy racing through me really isn't fair. I already knew that. And hell, I've fucked Logan. Still not my favorite thing to think about. "I know that, but they're twelve."

"How old were you," he keeps his voice quiet as he clarifies, "when you had sex the first time?"

I laugh, slamming the trunk down after retrieving the last bag. "You're really freaking."

"I'm serious."

I think about it. I had sex with one guy right before Logan. "Fifteen. Too young, but not twelve."

I watch his throat bob with concern and see it in his eyes as well. I know he was fourteen when he was at the Bradfords, and I want to comfort him. Tell him I know this subject isn't easy for him. But I'm silent and let him speak. "Kids like that . . . kids who never had a parent's love, who've been abused and tossed aside . . ." He stops for a minute, sounding pained, and I wish I could take it all away. His eyes lock on mine. "They have sex early. They're searching for that love."

I know there's no argument. I know Quinn, Sean, and Logan weren't the only kids he met along the way in the same situation. I know he knows what he's talking about. Hell, my parents didn't technically abandon me, and still, I gave my virginity to an older guy searching for the same thing. "I know, Rhys. Believe me, I know."

He seems to recognize that in me. "She's our responsibility. I don't want her getting knocked-up at thirteen."

"All we can do is show her how important she is to us, which is a big reason for this party. They're important to her, so they need to be important to us."

He nods decisively. "Okay, but they better not try anything."

I shake my head at him, laughing, unable to stop. "I like this protective side of you."

He acts like I'm the ridiculous one as we go inside, and they both help me decorate for her party. Soon after we finish, the boys show up at the front door together.

They're good-looking kids, a little rough around the edges with scruffy hair and ratty clothes, but I can tell they'll be handsome men someday. As I look at them, I imagine it's how Rhys looked at that age.

No wonder he's so worried.

We order pizza, and after we eat and sing "Happy Birthday" to her at my urging and she blows out the candles, we get them settled in the living room.

I bought three separate sleeping bags and have a ton of junk food ready to go as Bree searches for a movie on Netflix. They settle on a horror flick and then change into clothes for sleep.

I can feel Rhys's hesitance as they get settled in.

"Okay, you guys, if you need anything, we'll be right upstairs," I say as I take inventory of the snacks, deciding they have plenty.

I start toward the stairs, but Rhys isn't moving. "Those sleeping bags better be in the exact same spot tomorrow morning."

Bree looks horrified, but both boys nod their heads in understanding.

"Rhys." I'm at his side. "Let's go."

He watches them, still unmoving.

"Rhys," I keep my voice low because I don't want to embarrass Bree more, "come on. We need to let her have time with them."

He grunts something I'm sure I don't want to hear, but finally moves toward the stairs. We go into my room, and I close the door.

"Don't you think we should leave that open?"

I laugh and shake my head, slipping my dress over my head. "I thought maybe I could distract you."

His eyes take in every inch of my bare skin, and I don't have to say anything else before he quickly undresses, his body ready for mine. "No question tonight?"

I smile as I walk over to the bed, looking over at him as he stays by the door. "Hmm . . ." I think it over, and my mind goes to our conversation by my car. "How old were you?" The question escapes before I thought about it long enough to know not to ask. Because how fucking stupid can I be?

He was fourteen. I know he was.

My throat is dry as I croak, "Don't answer that. That was so stupid."

He walks to me. "Blair . . . you don't have to be careful with me."

I look into his eyes and feel even more like an idiot than before. He's impossibly strong and so damn beautiful, but I do worry about him breaking, of pushing him over the edge. "I don't want to hurt you."

"You couldn't even if you tried, Blair." His hand smooths over my bare arm, and the contact feels so good I tilt my head back.

My eyes flutter closed as his hand creeps between my legs, the wetness from the anticipation already there, and I smile when I hear him groan.

"You make me feel good, Blair."

"I'm sorry I asked a stupid question, Rhys." My head is still tipped back as his fingers slide through my wet folds, flicking over my clit and making my hips buck against his hands, chasing his touch.

"It wasn't stupid." I feel both hands on my hips before he spins me around and his hand flat on my back encourages me to lie down on the bed.

I oblige, lying flat, feeling excitement rushing through me when I feel him kneel behind me on the bed as I open my legs giving him room.

His large body covers mine, and I nearly jump out of my skin when I feel his lips brush over my bare back.

"I was fourteen when I had sex I actually wanted for the first time." I'm trying to concentrate on his words, but he's making it difficult when I feel his hard cock pressing between my legs and his lips on my neck.

The kisses he leaves there feel more intimate than anything we've ever done. "You were fourteen?"

I feel him nod against my neck, his hands on my hips as he lifts them enough for his cock to position at my opening and slide inside, driving me wild. I arch into him. His lips drag down to my shoulder. "Yeah. Right before I moved in with the Bradfords, actually."

My eyes close as I feel him move inside and feel relief that his first sexual experience was on his own terms. His body is pressed against mine as we remained joined. He plunges inside me and then takes his time pulling almost all the way out, teasing us both. I don't want it to ever end, but I know him being this close to another human is challenging.

"Are you okay, Rhys?" It's barely audible, and I smile when I feel his mouth dragging down my back before he drags his tongue on the same path and back up to my neck.

"I'm better than okay." He thrusts inside of me, and I moan loudly, pushing back against him, relishing in the close contact.

I should push up and let him have space, let him fuck me in full-on doggie style so he can have minimal contact, but I'm selfishly enjoying it too much.

I feel his hand move under my body and between my legs, finding my clit and causing me to squeeze tightly around him, pulling the sexiest groan from his throat. "Fuck, Blair."

"I'm close, Rhys."

I should probably try to be quiet, considering Bree has friends over, but I'm sure they have the movie up loud.

His teeth nip my shoulder as he fills me, hitting deep, one hand on my clit and the other finding my nipple. "Holy shit. Right there," I moan, wanting so badly to reach around and kiss him, but I don't push it.

I feel him jerk inside me right as my orgasm hits, both of us falling over the edge, his body fully covering mine.

I know I shouldn't get too comfortable, but I can't stop myself from hoping he'll fully let me in.

RHYS

"She hates this." I walk with Blair back to our cars in the parking lot of Bree's new school. There was a quick meeting we had to attend with her on the first day before classes start, and all I can think about is how miserable Bree looked.

She was wearing the school's jumper, and the kid does not like to wear skirts. If you ask me, it's fucking sexist as hell to make the girls wear skirts and the boys wear slacks.

She had fun with her friends this weekend, and now she looks so incredibly sad today.

"She'll be okay, Rhys. She's a tough kid."

I look at Blair and have no idea when she turned into this mom. It's exactly what she is though. She did everything she could to make sure Bree's party was perfect. She bought Bree presents she would actually want. She forced us to sing "Happy Birthday," and she's the reason Bree was smiling the entire weekend, right up until bedtime last night.

"I feel like a dick."

She just shrugs easily and unlocks her car that's parked right next to mine. "You are a dick."

I almost smile. "Thanks."

She laughs easily and opens her door. "Not for this though. This is protecting her. Soon we'll go to the hearing and get our kid. Then we can do anything we want. We can let her go to the school of her choice and know she's safe."

Now I do smile. It's small, and she may not even notice it, but it's there. This fucking woman actually makes me happy. Which then makes my heart squeeze with guilt because I know I can't ever be the man she deserves.

The night of the party in her bed . . . it took every ounce of control I had to let my full body rest against hers, to not pull back and bolt. To let my lips trail over her skin and breathe her in. She's this beautiful, perfect, strong woman with attitude to match my own, and I can't even lose myself in her long enough to look her in the eye when I fuck her. I can't kiss her lips and close my eyes, just letting everything go so I can be in the moment with her.

We both go about our day until I return to the school to pick up Bree. If possible, she looks even more miserable after school. She won't look at me when she walks to my car and climbs in the back seat.

"How was it?"

She doesn't look up to address me. "Fine. Dumb rich kids talking about the new iPhone all day long."

Not surprising. "You learn anything?"

She just shrugs her shoulders, and I hate how fucking upset she looks. This is definitely not what I wanted. To street kids, school can oddly be an escape, the place you're safest, the place you can be around your friends, have an actual meal.

School is something you hold close, especially in the earlier years before you find other stuff to numb your senses.

"What do you think Rhett and Fletcher are doing right now?"

Now her head picks up as her eyes meet mine in the rearview. "Probably starting their walk home."

"They don't ride the bus?"

She shakes her head. "They don't like the bus. We all used to meet and walk together. Until I moved in with them."

I don't miss the contempt in her voice when she says "them." I fight the sickening feeling in my gut. "Well, let's go see if we can find them."

She perks up. "Really?"

I smile inwardly, still not liking that her best friends are boys, but I know they're important to her. "Yes. Really."

I turn to go toward her old school, and it's not long before we see Rhett and Fletcher walking on the sidewalk by the school, both with bookbags slung over their shoulders. I slow to a stop and roll down Bree's window. "Hey!" she shouts happily.

They both recognize her voice instantly and jog over to talk to her. "Hey, rich kid," Rhett says, whistling when he sees her jumper.

I roll my eyes, and so does Bree. "Shut. Up."

He offers her a crooked smile, and I'm the next one to speak up. "You guys want to hang with Bree today? Will it be okay?"

They share a look, and Fletcher nods his head at me. "Yeah. That'd be okay."

I unlock the door, and they both climb in the back with Bree. If anyone saw this, they would probably call the cops. But I know the system, and no one is watching out for these kids, which again makes my stomach twist.

I drive them to get a snack at a drive-thru before driving

downtown to the shop. They camp out in the breakroom I have mostly finished now. I open the shop and shoot Blair a text to let her know we have three kids to feed tonight.

She writes me back immediately with laughing emojis and says I'm adorable.

I send her the middle finger emoji and then quickly get to work when a new customer arrives. Rhett seems particularly interested in my work, asking questions frequently, which I actually don't mind.

A couple of hours later, Blair breezes into my shop with that knowing smirk on her pretty face. I'm sitting behind the front desk, and she leans across it. "Did you adopt two more?"

I shake my head, glancing back to the breakroom where all three are watching television, Bree with a textbook on her lap. I turn back to Blair. "You're right. They're her constant. They ground her."

She smiles, looking into my eyes far too intensely, and I can tell she wants to kiss me. I want to let her, but instead I stand up and holler toward the back. "Your ride's here."

Blair rolls her eyes and stands up as Bree walks into the main shop area with the boys in tow. "Do we have to take them home?"

Blair shakes her head. "Hell, no. I haven't gotten to hang out with them yet." She flings her hair over her shoulder in her cool as fuck Blair fashion. "I thought we would go grab something for dinner and hang out at the house before I take them home."

Bree actually lights up. And I mean, the kid is beaming. "Okay." She turns to me. "Are you coming too?"

I shake my head. "I should probably keep the shop open."

"Maybe you should hire someone else to do that," Blair says, brushing past me as she heads toward the door.

"I can barely pay myself at the moment, Blair."

She just shrugs as the kids go and gather their things. "Maybe you don't have to worry about that, Rhys. I'll be your sugar mama." She winks, and I just shake my head, almost smiling.

"No thanks."

She laughs, expecting that answer. "You can pay me back in

other ways." She wags her eyebrows at me, and I shake my head, but this time I do offer a smile.

All three kids meet her at the door, and she opens it for them. "I'll save you a plate."

"Thanks."

She smiles at me before they all leave, and I think we can actually add this to our routine.

I'll do anything I can to make Bree feel comfortable with her new normal.

Blair

It's Friday, and we've had Fletcher and Rhett over all week after school. We agreed to let them stay the night again tonight, and Rhys has finally loosened up about the whole thing.

I was shocked when he told me I would have two extra kids to feed on Monday, but it's become our routine. They both assured me as long as they were back to their foster homes by nine, they were fine. And so far, there's been no backlash.

I did insist on asking both sets of foster parents Tuesday when I dropped them off and found out quickly they weren't kidding. None of them could be bothered with getting to know me or where the kids were spending their time.

Which infuriated me and sent a little relief through me at the same time because if they don't care, then Bree can still have her best friends in her life.

It's late when Rhys gets home, and the kids are already settled in the living room. I imagine he gave them a once-over before he came upstairs. I'm sitting on my bed, rubbing lotion over my elbows when he walks in.

"Hey." He looks tired. I know he's working his ass off at the shop to make sure the numbers look good for the hearing.

"Hi." His eyes soak me in, and I crawl toward him on the bed, shamelessly dressed in a lacey black teddy so sheer I know my nipples peek through.

"You could just wait for me totally naked." He approaches me slowly, and I wait for him to insult me or pull back, but what comes next is only his smooth, husky voice. "But this works too."

Again, I feel the caress of his gaze over my body, and I'm on fire with the anticipation as he sits down on the edge of the bed, not undressing.

I start to pout until he pulls a black box from his jacket pocket. "It's not much."

I sit up next to him, tucking my legs underneath me as he hands it to me. "You really got me a ring?"

I thought he was fucking with me or that he'd forget. I open the box, and a gasp falls from my lips when I see the beautiful wedding band. It's rose gold with small diamonds along it, with a dusty rose-colored jewel in the middle. "Rhys."

He rubs the back of his neck nervously, his eyes cast downward. "I know it's not a huge diamond. I guess it's morganite or something. But I don't know, it reminded me of a rose. And then the band was rose gold."

I want to kiss him. I stop myself, but God I want to. A tear slides down my cheek, one I curse because I hate crying. "You bought me a rose wedding ring."

He shrugs his large shoulders, still looking away. "I don't know why. I can take it back. I have the receipt."

I pull it out of the box and slip it over my ring finger. "Don't you fucking dare. Rhys, look at me."

He turns, his eyes meeting mine. "I love it. It's . . ." I sigh, looking down at the ring he took time to think about, the beautiful ring that symbolizes the tattoo he gave me. "Perfect. It's perfect, Rhys."

He smiles slightly at that. "Yeah?"

I nod my head and pry my eyes off the ring to look up at him. "Thank you."

He looks uncomfortable as he shrugs out of his jacket. "You're welcome."

I think about the band I ordered for him and smile to myself. "Yours should be here soon."

He nods his head, peeling his shirt off, his eyes moving from the ring on my finger to my teddy. "Okay."

I can feel his desire for me as I place the box on the bed and edge a little closer to him. "Are the kids watching a movie?"

He nods his head, standing up and popping the button of his jeans open. "Yeah. I made sure the sleeping bags were all appropriately apart."

I laugh. "I'm surprised you didn't measure the distance."

He pushes his jeans down, and my eyes travel over his naked body, going straight to his dick that's hard and standing at attention. Ready for me. "I thought about it."

He kicks his jeans off and rejoins me on the bed. I want to climb onto his lap, kiss him, and let him sink deep inside of me, but I know that's not what's in store for the night. I wait for him to take the lead. Something that's always been difficult for me.

"No question tonight?"

A stupid one comes to the forefront of my mind as I'm examining his package, and when his eyes meet mine, I know they gave me away.

"Go ahead."

I don't waste time asking because it's Rhys, neither of us really back down. "Why can't I say that you have a big dick? Most guys beg me to tell them how big they are even when it's an obvious lie." My eyes dart down to shamelessly ogle him. "Which with you, it's not."

He lets out a heavy sigh. "She used to tell me that. A lot." My gaze lifts back up to his face, and I hate the anguish etched there. "She would tell me how much bigger I was than her husband and how she couldn't believe it."

I want to joke about it. I want to help him move past it, but I tread lightly. "I mean . . . she wasn't wrong about you being big."

He doesn't smile, but he doesn't grimace either, so I'm calling it a win. But then his features darken. "She said it once when she was on top of me and he was watching." I watch him slowly swallow, it appearing to be painful. And I know he's lost in the memory. "I hoped he didn't hear it, but he did. And afterward he gave me the worst beating of my life. Broke two ribs."

That. Fucker.

Way to kill the mood, Blair.

"So, he had a tiny dick and was jealous of you. That's not your fault."

A small smile tugs at his lips, and then his hands wrap around the back of my neck, pulling my face to his before our lips crash together. It takes me a moment to realize what's happening. That Rhys is actually kissing my lips without me having to ask him to do it.

And God, it feels good.

I try to keep my hands at my sides, afraid I'm going to spook him as his hands grasp my neck and hold me to him. His tongue tangles with mine as we nip and suck, lost in the moment together.

He pulls his mouth away only slightly to breathe against my lips, "Touch me, Blair."

I suck in a deep breath of surprise from his words and bring my trembling hand between our bodies to graze over his taut abs, relishing in every single carved ridge. His lips attack mine again as we kiss, and I'm desperate for him. But I don't push him.

He pulls me to his lap to straddle him as we kiss, and I don't wait now, grabbing his hard cock and positioning it where I need him. When I sink onto him, we both groan deeply into our kiss, and neither of us relent.

I rock against him as his hands smooth over my back and mine explore his chest and stomach.

It doesn't take us long to get to the finish line, the experience a brand new one and jacking up the excitement for us both.

I can feel him tense a couple of times as he kisses me, almost like he's waiting for his mind to send him into a spiral, but when I come, he follows moments later, and we fall back onto the bed, me in his arms.

Will it last?
Who knows?
But I'll always remember tonight.

Rhys

Things have been going smoothly, far too smoothly. And I'm waiting for the massive fuckup that's on the way.

I look over at Blair, asleep in the bed, fully naked from last night. I've been sleeping in the bed with her lately. Ever since the night I gave her the ring, I've been trying to. I've been working on keeping my breathing even and letting her touch me.

Why?

I don't know.

Something about the way she looked at that ring set something off inside me. I could see the love she had for it. I was nervous as hell that she would laugh in my face, but the tears in her eyes and her admiring gaze twisted my insides in a good way, made me feel things I wasn't sure I could ever feel.

I stare at the band on my hand. It's simple. And it's rose gold.

She'd ordered mine before I gave her ring to her. And they match.

I don't know. That's gotta mean something, right?

The hearing is today, and I feel the anxiety rush over me as I sit here, staring at my wedding band, looking over at Blair, my wife. We've done everything we possibly can for it to go our way, but who the hell knows if it's actually enough?

I've never had the system work for me.

And if it does this time, then I'm going to be responsible for a minor. And it's permanent.

I nearly dart for the bathroom, the wave of nausea hitting me, but my phone rings on the bedside table, and I see Sean's name.

I grab it and answer gruffly, "Hello?"

"So, now you're fucking married? And not only that, you're married to Blair."

It's not a question, and Jesus Christ, Gillian has a big mouth. I groan and lean back. "Not for that long."

"Long enough, man. What the fuck? You were in my wedding."

I look over at Blair who is still fast asleep, and I want to tell him that it's just on paper. That it's not a big deal. But I'm not so sure that's the truth anymore, and Sean can smell bullshit from a mile away. "It was at the courthouse. Nothing special."

"Wow, man. You're all in now."

My heart squeezes tightly in my chest and beats at a steady thump, thump, thump I can hear in my ears. "I know."

"You still taking care of yourself?"

No. "Yes." I know he's talking about going to meetings, and the truth is I haven't been for a bit. I'm going to make time for it, but everything has been chaotic. I've been doing my best to make a profit at the shop by working long hours, and it's starting to pay off.

"Really?"

Again, he's a great bullshit detector. "I'll make more time for it."

"Okay, man. Well, I better be at your next wedding."

"Fuck you."

He only laughs because with us "fuck you" most definitely means we care. "Fuck you too."

I hang up and after placing the phone down, I run my fingers through my hair and try not to think about what will happen if Blair and I don't win custody of Bree today, if we have to pack Bree up and send her on her way with that motherfucker Herrington.

What I will do after that.

Because how the fuck can I not try to numb myself into oblivion if I know she's there under his roof? Where she doesn't feel safe.

Where everyone else assumes she has it made, but he has access to her every night.

A coat of sweat coats my skin, and my stomach lurches as I'm bombarded by so many fucking memories that I dart off the bed and just barely make it to the toilet in time.

"Fuck!" I flush the toilet and lean back against the wall, running my fingers through my hair and shaking like a pussy. Naked and cold. Numb.

Blair walks into the bathroom, wrapping a silk robe around her, but she doesn't say anything. She doesn't touch me.

She lets me sit there, leaning my head back against the wall, breathing in and out rapidly until finally my breathing starts to slow and my eyes close.

I want to be over this shit. I don't want to think about it anymore. Ever again. But it's something I'll never escape.

I hear the shower turn on. When I open my eyes, I see Blair's robe hit the ground at her bare feet. Then her hand reaches down for me.

She doesn't say anything, and I take her hand. She pushes the shower door open, and we both walk inside, the warm water hitting me first. I expect her to ask me questions. But she doesn't.

She just steps under the spray and washes her hair as I watch her in amazement. We've made a lot of progress even if we don't have a lot of contact when we fuck. Sometimes, I let her touch me.

Today, she seems to know I'm not in the mood to be touched. She keeps her distance as she washes, the suds falling over her immaculate body, and I'm frozen, still just watching her.

She smiles at me over her shoulder after washing her face. "We don't want to be late."

I nod in understanding as she allows me the spot under the showerhead, and I wash my hair. I face away from her and let the water run over my face, the liquid washing over me. But even though the water is warm, it's not enough to wash away the cold deep inside me.

I can't stop thinking about the what ifs, and I'm irrationally angry that Bree chose my shop to run into that day. Afraid of failure. Afraid of so many fucking things.

What if that was the worst decision for her? What if I fuck her up even worse than the Herringt— I can't even finish that thought. I know, without a doubt, that would have been far worse. And I love that fucking kid.

She's mouthy and strong. I'm fucking terrified of just how much I care about her.

"What if we lose?" It's a weak, quiet question that escapes my throat as I place my hands against the tile of the shower and let the water spray over me.

"We won't."

"We could. He has a shitload of money."

She's quiet for a moment. "Then we take Bree and head to Mexico."

I turn around to face her, seeing that smile on her lips that makes me ache with need. People think Blair's a bitch. They're wrong.

"I need to protect her."

She nods her head once, taking a deep breath. "We will. We have this, Rhys. There are no better parents for that little brat."

She's grinning, and I shake my head at her, fighting a smile. "You can't call her that there."

She laughs easily. "Will you move your big ass? I need to shave."

I laugh, turn around to make sure all the suds are gone, and then move out of the way.

"I like seeing that ring on your finger, by the way." She looks over her shoulder at me again as I push the door open.

I smile at her this time and wink. "Marking your territory?"

She nods her head assertively. "Damn straight."

I climb out of the shower and wrap a towel around my waist, letting her finish up. I want to go right back in there, plunge deep inside her and make us late, just live here in this safe space forever. But I know we have to go.

I have to face this head-on.

Blair

I HATE what today is doing to Rhys. I know it's tearing him up inside. There are so many things I want to say, but I don't. We drop Bree off at school. She spoke to the judge privately yesterday afternoon but won't be at the hearing. And now, we're on our way.

When I felt him rush toward the bathroom this morning, I knew his anxiety about today had manifested and left him physically ill. I wanted to comfort him. Instead, I gave him quiet and time. I know that Bree is just as anxious as we are.

I could see it in her eyes today, and I hate that she has to await her fate while she's at school.

When we arrive at the family courtroom, the Herringtons and their lawyer are already there, along with that bitchy social worker and the judge. I see Gillian is sitting with her husband on our side of the courtroom and smile at them as we make our way to the front.

The judge lets us know he's read the file. He's read statements from Ms. Winters and Gillian, which I didn't know was allowed but am grateful for, and then he asks us both to make a statement for our cases.

Mrs. Herrington goes on and on about how they can give Bree a wonderful life full of vacations and private schools, but I think it's apparent by our financials that we can match them on that front.

The judge thanks her, and then it's Mr. Herrington's turn. I feel Rhys's body tense beside me.

Please don't let him get sick in the courtroom.

"We fell in love with that little girl from the moment we saw her," his deep voice begins, and I take Rhys's hand in mine between our bodies. He jolts at first from the touch, but he doesn't pull away. "She came to us dirty and malnourished." Rhys's fingers squeeze tightly, and I grimace, but it's a pain I can stand. "We fed and clothed her. Had planned to enroll her in a private school well better than the public one she was attending." He sounds impassioned and angry as he speaks. It makes my stomach twist in knots. The way he speaks about Bree is as if she was their property that was taken away. "Why she acted out and made up lies, we don't know. But we still want her in our home."

Rhys's grip is almost unbearable, but I squeeze his hand back to let him know I'm there. Surely the judge can see through this sick asshole.

"I believe she has something special, and under the dirt and the grime is truly a stunning child."

Bile rises in my throat as I risk a glance at the judge, a man in his mid-fifties, with slicked back salt and pepper hair. He listens intently. "We fell head over heels for her and had plans, only to have everything ripped away by them." Mr. Herrington glares in our direction, and I stare right back, unwavering, and he continues. "I don't know why she would lie like she did, but we know she's a troubled child. We forgive her."

I cringe, not wanting to think about the ways he could punish Bree.

"Alright. Thank you, Mr. and Mrs. Herrington." Rhys and I both focus on the judge. "Mr. and Mrs. Moore, do you have anything to say before I make my decision?"

My knees feel weak, the realization hitting me that we could lose, and I speak up. "Yes. I do."

The judge nods his head at me. "Bree isn't troubled." My eyes dart to Mr. Herrington and then back to the judge. "She's exceptional. I've never met a person like her." I tuck my hair behind my ear and smile as my eyes meet Rhys's briefly. "Well, maybe one other person. My husband is like Bree. They were both children who were abandoned by the people who should have loved them the most. And we didn't pick her out like a puppy at the pound, she came barreling into our lives at the perfect time, seeking help and protection, from him." I pin Mr. Herrington with a hate-filled gaze and then look back toward the judge. "Rhys and I love Bree. We will take care of her and learn from her as well as teach her everything we can. We can provide her with everything she needs including the love not offered by her birth mother."

The judge watches me, listening as he nods his head. "Thank you." He turns to Rhys. "Do you have anything to say?"

Rhys clears his throat, and I know public speaking—hell speaking at all—is so not his thing. "Just that Bree deserves all the best. And she is the smartest kid I've known. And, for whatever reason, she wants us too."

The judge gives a clipped nod and then addresses us all as a whole. My heart is in my throat, and I can feel the perspiration on our palms as we hold hands.

"I have not taken this decision lightly. In fact, I've gone back and forth for some time over this case, and while it's clear you both have the best interest of the child in mind . . ." I feel Rhys's grip tighten, and I force myself to take a breath. "I did have time to talk to Bree yesterday. You're right," he gazes at Rhys and me, "she is extremely intelligent, and I find her competent enough for her opinion to be brought into consideration. She wants to live with the Moores. She was adamant about that. She sees them as her parents, and I won't tear her away from them."

A tear slides down my cheek at his words. And everything else is a blur as he makes it official.

Bree is ours.

She's safe, and she's ours.

The Herringtons throw a pissy fit, but we don't care. Rhys wraps his arms around me and hugs me tightly, and everything feels so damn right in this moment.

"Let's go break Bree out of school." I wipe another tear from my eye, and he laughs at me.

"I think this kid broke you. I've never seen you cry so much."

"Shut up," I say, but I can't stop smiling.

After filling out a shitload of paperwork, we go and pick Bree up early from school to give her the good news.

She actually cries when we tell her, real tears. And she doesn't even mock me for my own tears.

"So, does that mean I can quit the fancy school?" She looks up at us with adorable wide-eyed hope.

"We'll see," Rhys grunts as he opens the front door for both of us to exit the school.

I know it doesn't feel real to him, but it is. Nothing can change this unless we did something horrific, but according to the state of Missouri, Bree is our kid.

She shrugs. "Okay."

"You want to invite Fletcher and Rhett out for a celebration dinner tonight?" I ask her.

She nods her head excitedly, already pulling her phone out. "Sounds good to me."

I look at Rhys, my smile bright, but I see the darkness behind his eyes. I know today was hard for him.

Maybe I shouldn't have suggested dinner.

Rhys

GILLIAN AND HER HUSBAND, Phillip, joined us for dinner along with Rhett and Fletcher, and I know I should be on a natural high right now.

We have her. She's okay. She's legally our daughter.

And all I feel is numb.

I was so fucking happy in the courtroom. I even hugged Blair tightly to my body, but now, in the noisy crowded restaurant as Blair and Gillian talk about the future and Rhett and Fletcher give Bree a hard time about the fancy school she attends, it's like everything is blurry around me.

Listening to that motherfucker in court tell everyone what a saint he was. I can't stop thinking about the kids we didn't save, the ones out there in abusive homes, praying for anything to help them escape, whether it be their parents to come back, someone to adopt them who actually gives a damn, or even death. Because anything is better than that.

I'm happy Bree is with us. I'm happy she'll be safe, but I go back to when I was fourteen-years-old, and I feel like I'm going to puke.

"You guys had the good judge." I snap back to the conversation when I hear Gillian say that and look over at her. "When I saw it was Judge Martin, I breathed a sigh of relief. He's always fair."

Bree is smiling brightly as she sits in between her friends. "Yeah. He was nice."

Gillian gives her a kind smile, and Blair lifts her glass to take a drink before placing it in front of her. "Yeah, I was a little worried there for a second, seemed like he was buying Herrington's bullshit."

Now Bree looks worried as my eyes shoot to her. "Really?"

I see the fear in her eyes, the unmistakable nervous look. "Hey." My voice is directed only at her, and her eyes meet mine. "It doesn't matter. We. Won."

She gives a clipped nod, but I can tell she's trembling. Her voice is quiet. "I'm glad."

Blair offers her a wide grin. "As if there was any other choice," she smirks over at me on her left side, "besides Mexico."

I smile at that and nod, taking a drink of water. Bree smiles now and shakes her head. "You guys are weird."

Phillip laughs now, and it's odd how much he looks like Logan, or I guess Logan looks like him. And their laugh is similar. "You guys are parents now."

Everyone snickers, and we all start to eat. I start to feel my nerves calm, but then I jolt, almost embarrassingly so when I feel Blair's hand run up my thigh. I jump up out of my seat like she burned me, and everyone gawks at me, horrified.

Oh. Fuck.

My breathing is rapid, and I excuse myself quickly, escaping the restaurant and out into the cool autumn air.

I hear the door push open, and I don't look over because I know it's Blair. I can smell her perfume.

"Rhys. I'm so fucking sorry."

God damn it.

I look at her, seeing her expression and hating how afraid for me she looks. "Don't."

She shakes her head, the wind pushing her wild blond locks all over the place. She shoves it behind her ears and walks closer to me. "I'm sorry. That was so fucking stupid. I didn't mean—"

"To what?" I cut her off, feeling a fury that has nothing to do with her. "To touch your husband's thigh under the table? To fucking touch your husband?" I say the words in a calculated, slow fashion to show her that it's me who's acting crazy. Not her.

She shakes her head, tears in her eyes. "I know better."

I laugh bitterly. "You know better than to touch your husband? Do you hear how fucking insane that is? Do you get what you married yet?"

"I know exactly who I married, Rhys," she shoots back, deadly certain.

I shake my head. "You should be able to touch me whenever the fuck you want to, but you can't. You. Can't."

"I don't care. I'm just sorry I did it."

I shake my head, hating my fucking mind, my body, everything. "You shouldn't be sorry for touching me." I place my hand over my chest and look at her head-on. "I'm the freak. I'm the one who is so fucked-up. I saw the way he was in the courtroom today. I know that fucking look."

"You're traumatized by past abuse. It's normal."

Again, my bitter laugh fills the night air. "It's not normal. I'm not fucking normal. I'm fucked. Up."

Why can't she see that? She should take Bree and run far away, but I know she won't. She won't leave me. We're as good as really married in her eyes.

"I. Don't. Care."

"You deserve so much better than this."

She doesn't let the tears fall, and I can see how angry that makes her. "Don't say that."

"I'm so fucking sick of pretending, Blair."

I may as well have slapped her with the way she's looking at me. "Pretending?"

"Yes. Pretending." I take a step back from her, my blood boiling and revulsion rising. Repulsed by myself. "We have Bree now. She's not living with that motherfucker. We can stop this show."

"Why are you doing this?" She barely croaks the words, and I feel like my knees are going to buckle here on the parking lot pavement.

"I told you. You deserve someone you can touch, you can fuck, you can kiss."

"You've kissed me." I haven't since the night I gave her the ring. We've had sex in different positions, but I haven't actually kissed her lips.

"What? Twice? Once when you fucking begged me?"

She shakes her head at me, angry and betrayed by my words, and I know I'm being a dick, but I can't stop. I hate that I'm freaking out. But my body is on high alert from one mere touch on my thigh.

On a night that should be celebrated.

"I like your kiss."

I shake my head. "You shouldn't."

"Rhys, don't push me away." Her plea is a whisper and hits me deep in my chest.

"Let's just go back to dinner."

One single tear falls down her cheek as she nods her head, but she doesn't look triumphant. I know she's full of worry, and she should be. I can't ever be anything close to normal. I'm always going to freak out at the most obscure moments. The strangest things are going to trigger me, and she's going to have to clean it up and deal. It's not fair to her.

This is our reality.

Blair

WE MADE IT THROUGH DINNER, and I was careful to keep my distance. I know he's on edge. I know the hearing was hard for him, but I wish he'd let me in. After everything we've been through together, it stung when he said it was all pretend.

I know it's not.

After dinner, we drop the boys off at their respective foster homes, and Bree goes upstairs. I know she's happy we won. But she's a smart kid, and I'm sure she can feel the tension between Rhys and me.

"I'm going to the gym," Rhys says as he watches Bree's door close from where we're standing at the bottom of the stairs.

"Please talk to me." I know I sound weak, but I don't care. I'll be weak for him.

His head droops as he rests his palm against the door, facing away from me. "I can't. I have to go."

I hold back tears as he opens the door and leaves. When the door closes, I watch him back out of the drive through the window and try not to break. I don't think he's okay. I know he's struggling, and I shouldn't have let him leave.

Hours later, after lying in my bed and looking up at the ceiling through the dark, I hear the front door and don't waste time rushing downstairs. I need to make sure he's okay.

He's not in the foyer. Or the living room. I see the back patio door slightly ajar. My heart is rapidly thundering in my chest as I walk out the door, pulling it closed behind me. It's chilly out, the air crisp with the autumn cold, but Rhys is only in gym shorts and a cut-off shirt, his hair damp from the gym's shower.

"Rhys, you'll freeze out here."

He turns to look at me, his eyes almost vacant, and I yearn to see the fire in them. "You're one to talk . . ." His eyes skim my body since I'm only wearing a satin nightie.

"Well, let's go inside."

He sits on the pavement of the patio, and that's when my eyes drop to his hand, and I see he has a glass bottle in it, a whiskey bottle.

No.

"Rhys . . ." It's timid and hesitant, but it doesn't pull his gaze toward me. He only stares at the bottle which appears to be full.

"Don't," he begs me with his deep voice. "I just want it to stop. I want to forget." His chin lifts, and now all I see in his tortured eyes is agony. "Why can't I just forget?"

My heart splinters for him as I nod toward the bottle of alcohol that is literally poison to any addict. Like Rhys. "That won't help."

"It will for a little bit." He looks wild and desperate, like he's climbing out of his skin. "I can drink it and strip you naked, get lost. You'll like it. I'll be uninhibited and do anything you want. You can touch me, and I'll fuck you anyway you want."

I shake my head adamantly. I know he thinks I'm not fully satisfied, but I don't understand how he could think that. My body responds to him in every single way. "It won't be you. I don't want that."

He looks back at the bottle. "You can't stop me, Blair."

"Yes. I can." I take another step close to him and his eyes track the movement. "You aren't pretending with me." I lift my ring finger and his gaze darts to my hand. "This isn't fake."

He doesn't argue.

I kneel on the ground next to him, ignoring the cold. "I know it hurts. I know you're always actively hurting. I hate it for you." I reach out carefully, giving him time to realize my hand is going to touch his cheek. He still flinches as I make contact, gently brushing my hand over his stubble and turning his face so he's looking at me head-on. But he doesn't pull away. "Give me your pain."

"It doesn't work like that."

"It does, Rhys. Talk to me. Make love to me. Fuck me. Scream up at the sky with me. Cry with me. Break with me. So we can go ahead and put the pieces back together because I'm not going anywhere."

His chin drops, and I use my other hand to lift his face, my hands holding his cheeks as my forehead rests against his. "Blair," my name is a drawn-out rasp.

"I know. I can't imagine what it was like today in the courtroom, to hear him talking about Bree. I wanted to kill him."

He swallows tightly. "I hate that motherfucker. The way he talked about her. Like he was ready to groom her."

I cringe, thinking about it. "I know, but she's ours now. She's safe."

"So many aren't."

My eyes close as I rest against him. "I know."

His eyes lift, and I pull back enough to look directly at this beautiful man. "She used to touch my leg under the table at dinner." His teeth clench. "And other things. It was like her sick little game. Her fucking kids and husband were right there, and she would stroke my cock, like she was my lover, promising something more later."

"What a twat."

He snorts a quick laugh, and I swear it's the most beautiful sound I've ever heard. His hand wraps around the back of my neck, and he presses a quick kiss to my lips. "It always put so much fear in me, like he was going to see it and beat the shit out of me. Everything he did, it was with brute force."

It's so hard to picture Rhys being afraid of anyone or anything. He's so massive and strong, but thinking about his fourteen-year-old self, smaller and purposely malnourished . . . It makes me sick that there are people like them out there. "You're strong, Rhys. You always have been."

"I'm happy we have Bree. I'm glad she's safe, but you're fucked. You know that, right?"

I smile, my lips against his. "Happily."

His head shakes, but he doesn't move his lips from mine. "I want you to be able to touch me whenever you want to."

"So that means I have permission?"

"Always," he says effortlessly and lets my hand rest against his thundering heart.

"Good, but if you break," I love the feeling of his fingers curled around the back of my neck, holding me possessively to him, "do it with me. Don't ever run to anything else." My head swivels, and I look over at the bottle of whiskey.

He breathes deep, his lips ghosting over mine when I look back at him. "I promise."

I press my lips to his, and he doesn't wince this time, just kisses me softly. "You saved Bree today."

"You did." He nips at my bottom lip, his voice raspy. "And you saved me a long time ago," he breathes against my mouth.

He may think I saved him, but he gave me a purpose, saving me from a mundane, uncertain world.

Rhys

WHO THE FUCK *knew that Blair was my cure-all?* I mean, I'm clearly still fucked-up. Last night made that apparent. Buying that bottle of whiskey was stupid, but I just wanted to forget for a moment. To stop thinking about the horrific people that fostered me for two years.

But I knew deep down it wouldn't help. And there she was. Even though I was horrible to her at dinner, she was there. She's stubborn and fucking everything I never thought a guy like me could ever have.

And she held her ring finger with the ring I gave her proudly in the air and told me she wasn't going anywhere. It was at that moment that I knew I didn't want her to.

Not ever.

"Are you okay?" I look over to Bree, who's zipping up her jacket as we prepare to go to her school.

"Are you asking me if I'm okay?" I half smile at her. I'm working on it, but I swear my mouth isn't trained for the action. "I'm the adult."

She shrugs her shoulders. "That's debatable."

Fuck, I love this kid. "Funny."

She smiles brightly up at me, her curls everywhere. I think she wears it down like this, slightly messy, just to drive Blair crazy. I like it. Blair has tried to take her to a fancy salon to get it cut, but Bree refuses. "I am pretty funny."

"Why are you asking me if I'm okay?"

She puts her arms through the straps of her backpack and looks away. "You seemed . . . kind of upset last night."

Way to go, Rhys.

"I wasn't upset. I'm so fucking glad we won, Bree."

She looks at me cautiously. "You sure? I'm a handful. I know that."

I shake my head and put my hand on her shoulder. "No. You aren't, not even a little bit. But if you want to give this world hell, go for it. I encourage it." She smiles at that.

"So, what was wrong?"

I look at the clock on my phone and see we're about five minutes ahead of time. "Let's go out on the porch."

She nods and follows me to the porch swing Blair had me put up a couple of weeks ago. We sit down, and I let my feet drag along the concrete. "I'm really glad you're living here with us. And that it all worked out, but I wasn't sure it was going to. I was scared."

She nods, letting out a puff of breath, not looking at me. She stares at her feet. "I was too."

"Bree . . ." Her eyes meet mine, and I try to pull up all the courage I have. "Did he hurt you?" I swallow . . . and fight the revulsion. "I mean . . ."

"No." She doesn't make me say it. "I thought he was going to." I see tears pool in her eyes that kill me, but I let her speak. "He would get really mad at me sometimes and jerk me around. I had some bruises on my arms and stuff. But . . ."

I see the fear and disgust in her eyes. Emotions I recognize all too well. "It's okay. You can tell me anything."

She looks back at her feet. "He would whisper in my ear. Things like how pretty I was. Or how I was dressed like a slut." My fingers dig into my jean-clad thighs. "And he would brush his hand over my back and my arms." Her eyes lift, desperation in them. "I swear I never dressed slutty."

"It wouldn't fucking matter if you did." My voice is firm, too firm, and she flinches. I try to soften my tone. "It doesn't give him permission to make you feel uncomfortable. Nothing gives anyone that right."

She nods her head. "I could tell it was coming. I just felt it, and that day . . ." A tear slides down her cheek, and she quickly wipes it away. "That day I ran into your shop, he told me he was going to make me his. Legally. And I just knew . . ." She sobs, and I wrap an arm around her, letting her head rest against my shoulder.

"It's okay. You're here now, and I swear I won't ever let anyone hurt you."

I can feel her smiling. "I was running to Rhett that day. His real father works at the mechanic shop on your street, but I saw your shop, and I darted in." She looks up at me. "I don't know why."

I smile down at her. "I'm glad you did."

"Me too." Her honesty makes my heart clench with pride.

"Do you need to talk to anyone? Like a counselor?"

She shakes her head. "No. I'm okay."

"I get not wanting to talk, but surprisingly, it really helps."

She studies me carefully. "You were hurt."

It's not really a question, but I answer it like one anyway. "A lot." My voice falters, but I keep pushing through it. "My foster father beat the hell out of me. And then . . ." I'm tense. I'm sure she's afraid, but she rests her head on my shoulder.

"He really hurt you."

I nod. "Yes. He and his wife. They used me in every way. And they neglected me because they could. And they thought they could keep me weak." A small smile comes over my mouth. "But they couldn't. I got free."

"I'm glad."

"I'm still a little messed-up over it, but I'm healing." I shrug my shoulders. "You and Blair have helped."

"You guys have helped me."

"You want to leave that fancy school?"

She sits up straight and wipes her face. "I'm not sure. I miss Fletch and Rhett, but it's not so bad."

I smile at that, nodding my head. "Well, it's up to you. You just let us know what you want, okay?"

She stands up. "Guess I better get to school."

I stand with her and pull my keys out of my pocket. "I guess so. You can have your friends over tonight if you want."

"Thanks. I know they won't admit it, but they really like coming over here."

I shrug as we walk to my car. "They aren't so bad."

I drive her to school and then go to my shop, going about my day like I didn't have a full-on breakdown last night.

I expect to be haunted by memories all day after yesterday and then recounting it all to Bree today, but I'm in a surprisingly good mood until I get home in the evening. I decided to close down the shop to go home and eat dinner with the kids and Blair.

That sounds fucking crazy.

But I'm happy as I turn down the street and see a black car I don't recognize parked in front of the house. My eyes dart around, and I see Bree sitting on the porch.

That's not strange at all. She loves to hang outside and read. It's something she does often.

Fletcher and Rhett got into some shit at school today, and both had detention, so they were supposed to come over tonight.

But I don't see them.

I do see Herrington though. Standing in front of Bree with his fucking hands on her shoulders as she freezes in fear.

I'm out of the car in a flash and running up to them.

I'm going to kill this motherfucker.

Blair

A LOUD SCREAM makes me rush out the front door. I was trying to get a little work done and wait for dinner to be delivered, but the scream sends unimaginable fear through me.

When I open the door, I see Rhys on Mr. Herrington, raining down blow after blow with his heavy fist. "Rhys!"

I look over at Bree. "Are you okay?"

Oh my God. I didn't hear anyone pull up. I had no idea this asshole was here.

"Bree?" She looks down at the scene in front of us frozen. "Did he touch you?"

"Yes," Rhys growls as he lands another hit into Mr. Herrington's face.

"Rhys. Stop," I plead. "Don't kill him."

Rhys's fiery eyes meet mine, and I see the murderous gleam in his eyes. "He came to our home. He had her by the shoulders."

I turn back to Bree. "What happened?"

She shakes her head. "He said that he may have lost in court, but he would have me."

I want to tell Rhys to kill him, but I don't. I can't lose him. I look back to Rhys. "Let him up."

He shakes his head, still pinning him to the ground, his thighs straddling his waist, and that fucker isn't going anywhere.

"Rhys." I'm firmer this time. "If you kill him, you'll go to prison."

"It's where trash like him belongs," Herrington says before spitting blood out on the porch.

"Shut the fuck up before I remove your balls and kill you myself." I glower down at him, but then look back to Rhys. "I'm so sorry. I never in a million years thought he would show up here. I thought she was safe."

He's shaking. I can see his hands shaking, and I feel so damn guilty for not going out here with Bree.

"I'm twelve. It's not weird to let me be outside alone." It's like Bree heard my thoughts.

I look over at her, smoothing my hand over her cheek. "I should have been looking out for you."

"It's not either of your fault," Rhys grits out. "It's his." He glares down at Mr. Herrington, who doesn't look as scared as he should be.

"Rhys . . ." I place my hand on his shoulder, and he jerks it away, but I reach for him again. This time he leaves my hand there. "Let him up."

His breathing starts to slow as he looks down at him and then back at me and Bree. Finally, he climbs up and Herrington reaches his feet shakily, blood pouring out of his nose and trickling from his swollen lip.

"I'm calling the cops, you crazy deviant psychopath."

I laugh, "Go ahead. Call the cops and tell them that you showed up at our house and accosted a twelve-year-old girl. Please. Be my guest."

He looks at Bree, and I move my body between them shaking my head. He sneers, "She misses me. I wanted to assure her that I'd still be in her life."

"Over my dead body, motherfucker." Rhys is a hulk of a man on any given day, but today, my God, he towers over us all, his rage filling him out even more, dwarfing all others.

"Don't you ever come back here. I'll call the cops next time, or I'll just let him kill you." I fold my arms over my chest and stare him down.

Once again, he tries to look over at Bree, but Rhys moves closer to me, effectively blocking her from his predatory gaze.

"Leave," Rhys barks.

"I'll be back." Herrington starts down the stairs, but I can tell he's still dizzy from the beating.

Good, maybe he'll crash on the way home.

"I'll be here," Rhys promises.

He gets in his car and drives away before I take Bree's face in my hands and look down into her big blue eyes. "Are you okay?"

She nods her head in my hands. "Yes. I'm fine. Rhys got here right after he did. I was about to call for you."

I nod my head, glad that was in her plan. "Good. Scream loud. Hit him. Do whatever you have to if he ever comes close to you again."

"That's never happening again," Rhys grits out through clenched teeth, and his eyes meet mine. "She never comes out here alone."

I nod my head, and Bree pouts slightly. "I was fine."

"What if he would have taken you?" Rhys looks terrified now that Mr. Herrington is gone, and I feel the same fear.

Bree looks slightly worried, but she squares her shoulders. "I should be able to sit out on the porch. I can't be afraid of him forever, Rhys."

I see Rhys's throat bob, and I know he's at war with himself.

"Not afraid, but vigilant. You can hang out here, but someone should be with you. Fletcher, Rhett, Rhys, or me. We aren't such bad company." I smile.

"Okay," she huffs and turns to Rhys. "Okay."

He nods his head, semi-satisfied, but I know this is going to irk him. She goes inside, and Rhys takes a seat on the top step.

I sit next to him, my eyes examining his split knuckles. "Did you break your hand?"

He shrugs. "I don't think so." He flexes his fingers. "I can move them all."

"I'm so sorry, Rhys."

He shocks me when he wraps an arm around my shoulder. "Please stop apologizing. You didn't do anything wrong. Nothing."

"Are you okay?" My voice is shaky, and I hate it.

"Yes. It felt good to pummel him."

I laugh. "I bet. He had it coming."

"Yeah. He did." I lean on his shoulder, but I can feel his worry. "He's going to do it to another kid."

"Maybe you scared him."

"You know, right before I got sober for the last time, I overdosed." I turn my head so I can look up at his face. "It was bad. I woke up in the hospital. I almost died. I wanted to."

I hate hearing it, but I'm also so happy he's letting me in more and more.

"Quinn and Sean found me. They thought it was because Quinn was accepted to a school that was far away and maybe that was part of it, but really," he pauses and his words are laced with past pain, "really I'd finally found the courage to report the Bradfords. I told a social worker about them. And you know what happened?"

My stomach sinks. "I can guess."

"Nothing." He laughs bitterly. "I told them everything that happened in vague detail, but the beatings. I told them all about that. And barely feeding me. But I was told that the Bradfords were upstanding citizens and that kids were lucky to be brought into their world. Their fucking world."

"I'm so sorry the system failed you."

"I didn't want to live in a world like that, where kids are abused over and over, and no one protects them. I knew it would just keep happening, and there was nothing I could do about it."

"You saved Bree. I know it's not all of them, but one does matter, Rhys."

He hugs me closer to him. "Yeah. I'm starting to realize, Blair." His lips press against my temple. "You helped me see that. One does make a difference."

I feel relief pour through my veins. Because I believe him. I know he believes that. "She is going to go on to do good. And we did that."

He smiles. "Yeah. We did."

"I wish we could save them all."

"Me too."

So many emotions run through me, but the most prominent one is how much I love this man.

I don't say it out loud.

But I feel it. Everywhere.

Rhys

I FEEL on edge and jumpy, even if beating the shit out of Herrington was slightly satisfying. I'm angry that he showed up here in the first place and that the prick wasn't scared when he left. I held back. I wanted to kill him.

Maybe if Blair and Bree weren't right there, I would have.

I flex my swollen fingers as Bree sits on the couch next to Rhett, staring at her phone, worry in her eyes. She didn't seem frightened about Herrington coming back, but the fact that Fletcher hasn't showed up yet is definitely worrying her.

"I'm sure he's okay." I try to offer comfort before her wide, blue eyes lift and meet my stare.

"He wouldn't just ignore me."

Rhett shrugs, I think trying to make her feel better too. "Eh, he ignores me."

"That's because he doesn't really like you," Bree teases.

"Do you want me to take you over there?" I offer. My hand hurts like a motherfucker, and I really just want to go upstairs and get lost in Blair, but the concern on Bree's face is too much.

"You'll do that?" Damn it. She looks too hopeful.

I look over at Blair, who's already standing up from the couch. "Let's all go."

Rhett and Bree share a look, a secretive gaze between the two of them, and then Bree looks over at me. "He won't like us just showing up at his foster home."

Blair swings her designer bag over her shoulder. "I've already been there."

Rhett looks slightly annoyed, maybe a little embarrassed when she reminds them that she tracked down his and Fletcher's foster homes. Neither is in a great area.

"Come on. Let's go," I say, guiding them toward the door and out to my car.

When we pull up to the shabby neighborhood, poorly-lit and rundown, the first thing I see is Fletcher sitting on the cement stairs in front of a house. Damn it.

"Oh no." Bree's voice is quiet as she looks out the window at her friend.

It's cold out here, and the kid is only wearing a t-shirt and jeans with holes in them. I can see his breath in the light cast from the moon. "I'll be right back," I say as I'm already pushing the door open, but of course my little pain in the ass, Bree, is already out of the car before I slam my door shut.

We both walk up to Fletcher, leaving Rhett and Blair in the car. The kid is looking down at his feet and grumbles quietly, "Just go away."

"I'm not going anywhere." Bree sounds far too much like Blair when she says that and takes a seat right next to him on the stoop.

"Bree. You're such a pain."

I stand in front of them both. "You okay?"

He waves me off. "I'm fine. Just go."

"Let's see," Bree says it like they've been through this scenario before, and I struggle with my own demons as Fletcher raises his eyes to meet hers, showing off the shiner and split lip.

I wish I was surprised. I wish this sight, a twelve-year-old, skinny kid with bruises and blood on his face, was jarring to me. But it's not.

"God damn it," I seethe.

I see the tears form in Bree's eyes as she swipes her thumb gently over his swollen eyes. He hisses, but he doesn't push her away. "I'm okay, Bree."

She shakes her head. "You're not. You're not at all." She looks over at me, and somehow that one look fills me with pride. She looks to me for help. I guarantee you this kid doesn't like asking for help, but she knows she can come to me.

"We're leaving," I say, and Fletcher nods his head, wiping at his nose, and I see the blood on his hand.

"Good. I'll be okay."

I shake my head. "No." I gesture to Bree, him, and me. "We're all going."

He looks up at me, dark, intense eyes, jaded and already so damn tired at his age. "He'll kill me. It's past nine."

"He's not going to touch you." I look back at the car and see Blair's intense eyes prodding me for an answer, wanting to jump in herself, and then I look back at Fletcher. "We're going to the cops."

"What?" He stands up suddenly, shaking his head. "No. No, I won't do that."

"You have to, kid." I place my hand on my chest. "Believe me. You have to. You don't deserve this."

"They won't believe me anyway."

I point at his face. "Kind of hard to deny if we go right now."

"Please Fletch," Bree pleads with him and stands up, taking his hand, not exactly a fan of all the touching either, but I guess the kid needs some comfort. So, I press forward.

"Come on." I start walking toward the car, not giving him a chance to argue with me. I can hear Bree and him behind me and open my door, climbing behind the wheel.

Bree climbs into the back, and Fletcher follows. I hear Rhett's voice as I close my door and put the car in drive. "That asshole."

Blair glances in the back seat, and I can feel her weary eyes on me. No one says anything as I drive us to the nearest police station. Fletcher makes a report, and we get clearance for him to stay with us tonight.

After setting the kids up in the living room, Blair and I go upstairs. She closes the door and then moves silently to the bed, looking so goddamn numb it barely looks like her. Great, I'm really starting to rub off on her.

"Blair?" I sit on the edge of the bed, wanting to comfort her. But the day has been so fucking long, my nerves are shot, and I don't want to freak out from the contact.

"We can't save them all." Her words are breathless, and she sounds hopeless.

"No. We can't." I sigh, pushing my fingers through my hair. "But maybe we can save a few."

She looks over at me, her eyebrow lifted. "Like the few down in our living room?"

I shrug my shoulders. "We *are* certified to be foster parents."

She turns on the bed to face me better, tucking a leg under her. "You want to foster Rhett and Fletcher?"

I drop my hands to my thighs. "I don't know. Maybe."

"They're Bree's family."

"But they aren't related." And they're both boys.

She's thinking, I can see it on her face. Several thoughts are turning around in there. "It's like Sean, Quinn, Logan, and you."

"Not helping the case. Quinn and Logan are married now."

She laughs at that, letting her head tip back slightly. "You can't be afraid of Bree falling in love, Rhys. It's going to happen, and she already loves both of them. It would be normal for that to morph into real love someday."

I cringe at that thought, wanting her to stay young forever. "Maybe we'll just care for them until they can find a nice home to run out puberty."

She laughs again. "You aren't keeping them apart even if they aren't living together."

"You really think she's going to date one of them?"

She slips her top off, letting it fall to the floor. "Maybe. Maybe both. Maybe neither. I don't know. I just know you can't stop it."

"So, we're going to do this?"

She smiles, nodding her head instantly, and I can tell she's already sold. "Let's rescue some kids. Do some damn good."

"Okay, Blair."

She's beaming now as she crawls to me over the bed. "Now, get naked."

I grin, liking her hungriness for me.

Something I used to fight but don't think I will ever again.

Rhys

THANKSGIVING and Christmas have come and gone. We've had Rhett and Fletcher in our home since we found out Fletcher was being abused. We have long-term care licenses, and although the social worker—not Ms. Winters, thankfully—checks in occasionally, everything has been smooth.

We, okay Blair, offered to pay for the boys to go to private school, but they both declined. Surprisingly, Bree has stuck there. I think it was easier for her to make that decision now that she can come home to the guys.

I'm just finishing with a customer when the door dings open, and a kid who can't be over eighteen walks in. "I'll be with you in just a minute."

I take the payment from the guy with a fresh tattoo, and he thanks me before leaving. I turn to the kid, and I feel like I've seen him somewhere before, but can't place him. "Hey, Rhys."

His dark hair is shaggy, and his clothes are tattered, but he's a good-looking kid. There's a smirk on his face as his green eyes meet mine. "Christian?"

His smile widens. "Yeah. You remember me?"

I nod. We grew up in the same area. I'm five or six years older than him and haven't seen him since I was eighteen, but yeah, I know him. "Yeah. Charity's little brother."

He nods again. "Yup, that's me."

Charity is a couple of years older than me. They moved into the hellhole right before I left. "Are you okay?"

He just laughs, sitting down on the bench I have for customers. "I'm fine. Just looking for a job."

"Here?"

He shrugs. "If you'll have me."

He's acting cool, but I can tell he's desperate. "Are you eighteen yet?"

He nods. "Yesterday."

"Okay." The shop has been turning a profit lately, and I can afford someone to help around here, especially someone who needs an out as badly as I'm sure he does. "I'll hire you. You have a place to stay?"

"I'll find somewhere."

I look up. "There's an apartment above this place. If you're working here, it's yours."

"Thank you, Rhys."

I offer him a quick nod, uncomfortable with his thanks, feeling like it's the least I can do for this kid, one of the kids left behind in that fucking house.

I swallow tightly, bile rising in my throat wishing away memories and guilt. "How's your sister?"

He visibly tenses and shakes his head. "I don't know. I haven't seen her for a while. She bailed as soon as she turned eighteen."

"Jesus." I want to ask him so many things, but his eyes are pleading with me not to.

I'm almost certain when he says bailed, he means from the Bradfords. He was only eleven when they took him and Charity in. Seven years. Seven fucking years in that house of horrors.

My blood runs cold, and I ache from the inside out. "I'll show you your new home."

He forces a smile, but I see the pain he pushes deep down. I want to tell him he's going to be okay, but I don't fucking know that.

All I know is I'm going to do everything I can to make sure he is.

After getting him settled and giving him some cash to pick up some things he may need, I go home to Blair. I'm tense and angry. The guilt inside me is threatening to swallow me whole.

I should have tried harder to get them all to believe me. I knew other kids were there. I knew Charity and Christian from school and a group home before the Bradfords. I knew them. And I let them suffer.

Blair is on the bed, tucked under the covers, but she has her iPad on her lap and looks up at me with a smile. "Finally."

"Miss me?"

She nods her head, her ring glistening on her finger like a beacon for me to join her, to be near her. My heart knows she's the only thing that's going to make me feel any better. I kick my shoes off and climb onto the bed, glancing at her screen and seeing she has a real estate site up. "Looking for a new house?"

"I think we need a bigger house."

I shake my head and tuck an arm under my neck. "Why? So we can collect more kids?"

"Maybe." She shrugs. "I like it. And the ones we have could probably use a little more room."

Right now, the boys are sharing a room, and Bree has her own. "You're crazy."

Doesn't bother her, and I admire the fuck out of Blair. "I like the idea of saving several little Rhyses."

"I told you I don't like that nickname." She laughs, ignoring my broody ass.

She doesn't have to do any of this. She didn't have to marry me and adopt a kid. She didn't have to take in foster kids. But she wants to. She wants to be the good in the world. And she is.

Her hand rakes through my hair, and I only smile at the action. No wincing. It feels good. "What's wrong?"

She always knows. "A kid from my past showed up at the shop, wanting a job."

"Did you give it to them?"

I nod. "Yeah." I look up at her. "I guess I want to save some kids too."

She smiles at that, big and full of hope. "Good. Are they okay?"

"He's fine. I guess." I swallow the pain down, closing my eyes and letting her stroke my hair. "He lived with the Bradfords."

"Oh shit," she breathes.

"Yeah."

She puts the iPad down and lays her head on my shoulder, curling her body to mine, and I let her fill in the piece of me that's been missing as she presses against me. "It's good that you gave him a job then. You'll be the perfect boss."

"I don't know if I'm strong enough for it, Blair," I admit it begrudgingly.

"You are. You're the strongest person I know."

I turn and press a kiss to her temple. "That's you, Blair. You are, without a doubt, the strongest person either of us know."

"I told my dad we're married." Her hand slides over my t-shirt, over my chest.

"Wow. How did that go?" She doesn't talk to her dad often, and when she does, it's usually about business from what I've gathered.

"Fine. He was pissed I didn't get a prenup."

"I don't want your money."

She laughs, her finger tracing over my pec. "Oh, I know, but it's yours if anything happens to me, regardless." She tugs at the hem of my t-shirt. "I really want this off."

I lift up and oblige, pulling it up and over my head, tossing it to the floor. "I don't want your money."

Her finger swirls over the tattoo on my chest and then down the sleeve of tattoos on my arm. "I don't really care, Rhys. You're my husband. If something happens to me, I want to make sure Bree, Rhett, Fletcher, and you are okay." Her finger slides down the middle of my abs, following the carved muscles. "The house is in my name so we can sell it and get a bigger one. The trust is also in my name. And I've put both in your name also, along with college funds for all three kids."

She knows I don't give a damn about money, but the thought that she's planned that far ahead does something to me, something crazy. I like planning for the future, but I can't imagine one without her in it. "So, we're like, really married, aren't we?"

She just snorts a laugh at me. "You're an idiot." I smirk, and she kisses the corner of my mouth where it's curving up. "Yes. I think it stopped being for show a long time ago."

"Or it never was," I say, looking down into her eyes.

"Yeah." She kisses my lips. "Maybe it never was."

It never was.

Blair

I LAY next to Rhys and look out the window. It's still dark outside, not even morning yet. But so many thoughts are running through my head. I worry that Rhys hiring someone from his past will hurt him, but I'm so damn proud of him for helping that kid.

I want to save them all.

I'm guilty of that.

The house I have my eye on has six bedrooms, and I'm already thinking about how we could possibly take in two more kids who need a good home. Bree, Fletcher, and Rhett are all safe. It would be good to move though, so that fucker, Herrington, can't find Bree. Still, we keep a close eye on her, and I know Rhett and Fletcher do the same.

Let him try to get near her. It will be the last thing he ever does.

I can also feel how tense Rhys is as he sleeps. He rarely sleeps peacefully, and I'm not sure he ever will. But he does let me touch him more and more. I would love to help him relieve a little tension, pull down the covers and take him into my mouth, but I don't think that would go over well yet.

I hate what that fucking bitch took from him, but it doesn't matter. I know it doesn't. I have Rhys, and I love every single thing about him.

It was never for show. I've loved him since the first night he couldn't fuck me. He felt like he was using me, but he's truly the only person who's ever made me feel useful.

"You're staring." I hear his voice rumble, and I jump in surprise.

"You're awake?"

"You're staring. I can feel you."

I feel slightly bad about that, wondering if I spooked him. My voice is raspy and meek when I ask, "Did you think it was her?"

He laughs and the sound is beautiful as he pulls me to his side. "No. I didn't."

"You can tell me. I'm sure it's still hard waking up next to me." I feel a stupid girly tear slide down my cheek and onto his bare chest.

"Why are you crying?"

"I hate what she took from you. I hate that I'm never going to be able to wake you up in a sexy fashion because of what that bitch did to you."

He holds me closer, which makes me smile. "I knew it was you and not her, Blair. You smell different."

"What?" I look up at him.

"She had this really expensive perfume. It almost smelled clinical." His hand strokes my back. "Yours is kind of sweet. I like it."

I look down again, barely able to make out his taut abs in the dark. "You know the difference?"

"Yeah. I do."

"I hate what they did to you, Rhys," I choke through the tears that fall. "But I love everything about you." I look up at him again and wipe the stupid tears from my face. "Everything."

"I love you, Blair." I gape at him, the words causing my heart to squeeze. "You made me like myself again."

"Just like? Not love?"

"I'm working on it. I did a lot of shitty things when I was high or drunk, things that make it hard to like me. But I'm getting there."

There's nothing he could do to make me not love him, but I'm grateful for him staying sober. "I get that. I spent a long time building up my bitchy persona and not liking myself very much either."

"I love everything about you too." He dips his head down, his lips nearing mine as he growls, "Badass Barbie."

I roll my eyes but smile and give him a quick kiss as his hand swipes over my side and up to my breasts.

"So, tell me about this rose."

"From Beauty and the Beast."

"I know that, but I've still never seen it. What's the role of this rose?"

I smile to myself. "He was once a handsome prince who had a curse put on him to make him this beastly creature. Unlovable. But he had to make someone fall in love with him before the last rose petal fell."

"Did he?"

I nod. "Yes."

His mouth is still on mine, and I crave him, every single part of him. "And then what?"

"Then he turned back into the handsome prince, but you know what I think, Rhys?"

He flips so my body is safely tucked under his as he looks down at me, and I slide my hand over his hard stomach. "What?"

"I think he was always loveable. Always that man." He leans down and presses a kiss to my cheek, and then the other. "She just had to remind him."

His lips press to mine softly. "Sounds like a lucky bastard."

I grin up at him and cup the back of his neck, keeping him close to me. "So was she."

Our love story wasn't easy. It doesn't end here. There will still be struggles, but as far as I'm concerned, as long as I have Rhys by my side, we will live happily ever after.

THE END

BONUS CHAPTER

Rhys
Six months later . . .

"Hey boss . . ." Christian peeks his head into the private room I'm working in, careful to keep his eyes only on me, being professional as I demand. The chick requested a private room, wanting a tattoo of her lover's name under the belt.

"What's up." I look up and see his face is pale. "What's wrong?" I stand up, placing my tattoo gun on the tray, walking to him.

He keeps his voice low. "Mya's here."

I quirk an eyebrow in surprise. "Mya? Why?"

He shrugs. "She didn't say. She's looking for you though, and it can't be good."

A cold, bad feeling runs over me as I tell the customer I'll be right back. She nods an okay and continues flipping through her phone as I walk out front and immediately see Mya. She's older now, more grown up than the last time I saw her, and the hairs stand up on the back of my neck.

She's dressed in all black, her brown eyes sparkling, but I see the deep-seated pain in them. The pain that was always there even at

BONUS CHAPTER

nine-years-old, when I first met her. I was twelve, and we wound up in the same temporary foster home. Her baby brother and her. Now her black, curly hair is pulled up into a loose ponytail, and her black dress shows off her new figure, but to me she's a kid. She's definitely grown into a beautiful woman.

She's Charity's age, and I kept an eye on them both until I left. Left Charity and Christian in that house. Left Mya and her little brother in the shitty neighborhood we all grew up in. Left Sean, Logan, and Quinn, trying like hell to escape from it all, but now everything has come full circle.

And I need to know why she's here, even if I don't want to hear it.

"Mya," I breathe.

She looks me up and down, and I can tell she's tired. From lack of sleep or just life, I'm not sure. Probably both. "Rhys. You grew up."

I nod. "You too."

She bites her bottom lip and looks around, her eyes taking in everything, and I grow apprehensive every second that ticks by.

"Are you okay?" It's a question I already know the answer to. If she were okay, she wouldn't be here. You don't track down your past when you're okay.

She ignores the question, her eyes still sweeping throughout my shop. "It looks like you're doing well, Rhys."

I fiddle with the wedding ring on my left finger as I look around the shop that's fully finished out and thriving. I'm probably going to have to give in soon and hire a tattoo artist or two to keep up. "Yes. How did you find me?"

"It wasn't hard." Her eyes narrow on mine. "I had Sean's number. He told me where to find you."

I give a clipped nod, not surprised. Sean and Quinn both watched out for Charity and Mya also. Really, there's a code with street kids like us. We look out for our own. "What's going on?"

She looks away, and I see the tears forming in her eyes and feel like I might puke.

BONUS CHAPTER

"Mya," I prod, needing an answer.

Her brown eyes meet mine. "I came straight from the funeral . . . Rhys . . ." Her voice is strangled, and all I see is that scared little girl she was all those years ago. She held her head high, but she had big, fat tears in her eyes when the social worker dropped her and her little brother off. She wanted to be brave for him, just a baby herself at the time, but she still knew how much he needed her, how worthless their junkie mom was.

"Who died?" I ask.

Her bottom lip quivers, and she barely croaks out the answer. "Trey."

No. No. No. I walk toward her, my stomach clenching. Trey. Her little brother. No. I would have bet anything it was her junkie mother who checked out, but her brother? Her fucking brother. "Trey?" I shake my head. "He's what? Eleven?"

She holds back tears as she nods her head once. "He was. And it's all my fault, Rhys."

I pull her into my arms, holding her body to mine and comforting her like the little sister she is to me.

Eleven.

He was eleven-years-old, and now he's dead.

"I'm sorry," I breathe.

Because I left them behind.

NOTE FROM THE AUTHOR

Thank you so much for reading! I hope you enjoyed Blair and Rhys! Their story certainly meant a lot to me! I take this subject extremely seriously. I want all children to be safe and cherished.

Thank you to everyone that made this book possible! Ari, Emma, Elle, Jeanna, Dena, Elizabeth, Veronique and Wildfire Promotions! You all mean the world to me!

Thank you to all the bloggers, Bookstagrammers, readers and especially the Novelties!

And thanks to my baby girls and the love of my life. Thanks to them for putting up with my sleep deprived cranky self!

If you or anyone you know is suffering from abuse, please get help. The shame should lie only with the abuser and never with the victim. Reach out because I swear to you, someone cares. I care.

Love you all!
Nicole

Made in the USA
Columbia, SC
19 April 2022